PRAISE FOR GUARDIANS UNLEASHED SERIES

"Jerusha Agen once again delivers top-level suspense and thrilling action. *Covert Danger* kept me looking over my shoulder and flipping pages. Fast-paced suspense at its best."

DIANN MILLS, BESTSELLING AUTHOR OF
CONCRETE EVIDENCE ON *COVERT DANGER*

"Hang on! This action-packed story doesn't let up until the good guys win!"

NATALIE WALTERS, AWARD-WINNING AUTHOR OF
LIGHTS OUT AND THE *HARBORED SECRETS SERIES*
ON *COVERT DANGER*

Hidden Danger kept me reading and on the edge of my seat from page one through the end. Jerusha Agen writes a gripping suspense filled with danger, romance, and K-9s complete with a strong faith thread.

MIDNIGHT CLEAR

BOOKS BY JERUSHA AGEN

GUARDIANS UNLEASHED SERIES

Midnight Clear (prequel novella)

Rising Danger (prequel)

Hidden Danger

Covert Danger

Unseen Danger

Lethal Danger

Terminal Danger

SISTERS REDEEMED SERIES

If You Dance with Me

If You Light My Way

If You Rescue Me

MIDNIGHT CLEAR

GUARDIANS UNLEASHED  A PREQUEL NOVELLA

JERUSHA AGEN

SDG Words, LLC

To my grandma, Marion. I didn't know you long enough, but the memory of your strength, intelligence, and love lives on.
Thank you for loving me.

Soli Deo Gloria

In love he predestined us for adoption to himself as sons through Jesus Christ, according to the purpose of his will, to the praise of his glorious grace, with which he has blessed us in the Beloved.

– Ephesians 1:4b-6

ONE

The Christmas carol blaring from the TV choked as darkness swallowed the house.

A booming *woof* sounded behind Marion, making her jump. She turned but could barely decipher the outline of the 180-pound St. Bernard who continued to bark by the sofa.

"It's okay, Herc. Just a power outage." A warm nose nudged Marion's hand, and her fingers found Lily's scruffy head. The seventy-five-pound mixed breed dog kept her chin on Marion's lap, clearly wanting to stay comfortable on the sofa.

Hercules moved closer as he barked, the loud sound ringing Marion's ears. "We better show Herc it's okay, Lily."

The sweet girl lifted her head and hopped off the sofa, ready to follow Marion as she stood.

"Herc, that's enough." She found her way through the dark, her eyes adjusting to let her locate the big dog and rest her hand on his broad back. "There's nothing wrong. The lights just went out."

His next bark quieted as he fidgeted under her touch.

"How about we go for a walk?" That should give him

something else to think about beside the fear that caused him to bark at seemingly everything, real or imagined.

And with the blizzard that was supposed to hit after this first snowstorm, she'd better not waste any time getting the generators up and running. The kennel would come first. The thought of not having power for the twelve dogs she currently sheltered at Forever Home made her shudder.

She quickly bundled up, throwing a down-filled jacket over her Christmas-patterned fleece pajamas and shoving her cozy-socked feet into winter boots. She added a scarf in case she got lost out in the storm, heaven forbid.

Slipping harnesses on Lily and Herc and gloves on her hands, she opened the front door.

Her jaw dropped. The weather forecasters hadn't been kidding when they'd said this storm would bring several feet of snow overnight. At least a foot of fluffy white powder greeted her in front of the door on the front porch, and the snowfall was predicted to last until late tomorrow, Christmas Eve.

Herc barreled through the door ahead of Marion, pulling her eagerly. She laughed. "Okay, slow down, buddy. I know you love snow, but you have to stick with me right now."

Lily followed at Marion's side as they trudged through the deep snow, letting Hercules stay out in front and gulp mouthfuls of flakes as they walked. The two stairs that led from the porch to the ground were completely buried. And it was a good thing she knew where the path was that led from her house to the kennel because there was no trace of it now.

She slipped her wrist through the loop of Lily's leash so she could pull out the flashlight from her pocket and switch it on. Although it was surprising how much she could see without the artificial help.

She'd forgotten how reflective snow was, creating its own

light. But the fluffy flakes falling in a thick curtain from the sky ensured visibility stayed low.

Thank goodness she didn't need to drive anywhere in this weather. Snowplows probably wouldn't even start clearing the rural roads by her house until the storm was over.

She never really needed to go anywhere anyway. Except where the rescue of a dog was concerned. Hopefully, any strays out here in the country or in the Twin Cities would be able to find shelter tonight. At least she and Lily had found two of their newest residents on the streets of Minneapolis last night before this storm hit.

"Let's hold it here, guys." The unlit security light above the kennel's front door offered no help as she pulled keys from her jacket pocket and tried to find the right one.

A noise drew her head up.

Was that a crunch? Like someone walking in the snow?

She shined her flashlight past the building to her left, then back toward the house, illuminating only a shower of snowflakes as beautiful as the ones in the final scene of the movie she'd been watching when the power cut. Too bad the outage turned off the Christmas lights she'd decorated her house with, too. The multi-colored lights would add so much cheer and form a perfect Christmas picture with the snow. Then she'd be back to imagining romance instead of scary noises in the dark.

Hercules had a better imagination for scary than she did, anyway. He'd have told her if there'd been any real noise.

She turned to the door again and pulled off her clumsy thick glove to better catch the right key in her fingers. Cold air chilled her skin as she inserted the key in the lock and twisted the freezing knob. But the low-twenties temperature of tonight would be nothing compared with the arctic winds that were supposed to blow in tomorrow on Christmas Eve.

Or today, technically. The clock had just passed midnight

before the power went out. At least that was the time she'd figured it would be when she'd decided to watch another Christmas romance before going to bed.

Well, merry Christmas Eve to her.

"Herc, with me."

Lily hurried inside the kennel beside Marion, but the St. Bernard lingered for a few more gulps of snow.

"You'd think I never give you any water to drink." She grinned at the big boy's square face as he munched his favorite frozen treat. "Come on, buddy."

He lumbered inside and promptly shook his whole body, scattering wet snow everywhere, including Marion's cheeks just as she took off her scarf. She chuckled. "Thanks a lot, Herc."

A few barks and whines echoed in the large room of kennels that lined the far wall.

"Hey, kids. Sorry to wake you all up." Her gaze traveled with her flashlight beam over the dogs of various sizes, breeds, and mixes. She didn't approach their half-carpeted kennels she'd outfitted with cozy dog beds since this was their normal sleeping time. They didn't need to get excited about her presence and think she was going to play with them. Her quick scan saw nothing amiss, and their doggy doors shouldn't be blocked by snow thanks to the roof over the outer runs.

Keeping Lily and Herc on leash instead of letting them loose inside as she usually did, she went to the storage room. She put the dogs into a down stay while she pulled out the new generator.

How crazy was that timing? Only this summer, Phoenix Gray had pushed Marion to do more fundraising and had shared her connections to put Marion in touch with people eager to support Forever Home's effort to rescue and rehabilitate dogs for adoption. Phoenix's fund drive and donors had provided for the roof over the outer runs and two generators —one for the kennel and one for the house.

Marion suspected Phoenix may have donated one of the generators herself, but Marion wouldn't dare ask. Couldn't risk pushing away her only volunteer who had also turned into a fundraising wizard.

Reminding Lily and Herc to stay with her, Marion managed to get the generator outside. The snow presented a bit of a problem, but the outdoor power box she had to plug the generator into was only a few feet from the front door.

Didn't take Marion long to go back inside, grab a shovel, and clear a path to pull the generator closer to the power box. The dogs cheerfully went along with her back-and-forth trek, Herc clearly overjoyed every time they returned to the snow. Lily stayed near Marion naturally, as usual, always ready to do or be whatever Marion needed.

Starting the generator was a bigger challenge than Marion had expected, though Phoenix had warned her. Marion had thought she'd have no problem with it since she was usually good at mechanical things.

She gritted her teeth as she tried for the third time to get the generator to start. She yanked the cord. It sputtered and quit. Again.

She straightened and pulled her scarf away from her face as the exertion of trying to start the beast heated her body. What a way to spend the night before Christmas Eve. Hardly the Christmas festival complete with hot chocolate, dancing, and romance featured in the movie the power outage had rudely interrupted. The hero had just declared his love and was about to kiss the heroine.

Marion knew the kiss was coming since it did at the same moment in all the other Christmas movies she'd watched every night this December. Including the other two she'd viewed tonight before the unfinished movie.

She never should've stayed up so late to watch three in one evening. She knew better than that, given how early she had to wake to take care of fourteen dogs. But she was determined to enjoy this Christmas. Not succumb to depression like every other Christmas of her life.

She tugged the generator's cord again. Still wouldn't catch.

At the beginning of December, the movies had been fun, conjuring the warm fuzzies of Christmastime she hoped would help her enjoy the season the way other people did.

But now every time the closing kiss filled the screen and the credits rolled, a sinking feeling sucked the fuzziness right out of her. And she was left with the usual. Loneliness.

Maybe it was like the characters in these movies usually said to their single friends. Without someone who loved them, they weren't really living.

Marion swallowed. Stared into the shower of wet flakes. If she wasn't really living, then why live at all?

Something pushed her gloved hand.

Lily. Marion knew it was her girl before she looked.

White snowflakes fell on Lily's head, sparkling on the patches of scraggly brindle fur and instantly melting on the other side of her face where bare gray skin with jagged dark lines evidenced her unhappy past.

Marion placed her hands on the contrasting sides of Lily's face and bent to kiss the rough fur on top of her head.

Marion took in a deep breath as she straightened. She didn't need to think like that anymore—to question if she should keep living. Lily needed her. The other dogs needed her. The ones here now, the ones she'd saved before, and the ones she would rescue in the future. She had a reason to keep going, even if no man would ever—

A bark burst out of Hercules.

Marion startled. "Honestly, Herc. Do you have to do

that?" She leaned over the generator and gave it another try. It caught and kept going. A smile stretched her mouth. "We did it, guys!" She clapped her gloved hands together.

Herc didn't seem to share her excitement. The big furry beast launched a string of *woofs*.

Her smile faded as her brow furrowed. He didn't usually bark in a long sequence like that.

He stood still as a statue, his tail tucked as he stared into falling snow and darkness beyond the corner of the building.

Even Lily looked in the same direction, her body language signaling she was curious, though not afraid.

Tension clenched Marion's chest.

How silly. As if anyone or anything dangerous would be out in such weather.

But her instincts didn't listen.

Trying to let logic prevail, she forced calm into her voice. "It's fine, Herc. Nothing's there." Though he clearly wasn't going to be able to relax until she proved it to him.

She took in a breath, gathering her slipping courage. She was the adult here. "Okay, let's go check it out."

She started forward into the unshoveled snow with Lily. Herc's leash tightened, making Marion stop. The St. Bernard stayed rooted in his spot, still barking.

"Herc, I'm sure there's nothing there. Let's go, buddy. Don't you want to see? With me." She reached into her pocket for his favorite treat and gave it to Lily.

Marion grinned as the leash slackened, and Herc came close. "Oh, you want one of these, too, huh?" But just as she handed him a treat, he stiffened again and barked, letting the food drop from his mouth.

Good grief. She had to find out what was there, or she'd never get back inside tonight.

Pretending her pulse wasn't starting to race, she calmly

encouraged and cajoled Herc to get him to follow her to the corner of the building.

She cautiously peered around the blue siding. What if Herc was right and there was something dangerous th—

Her gaze caught on a dark mound in the snow.

Her breath stopped.

She aimed her flashlight at the object. A jacket? She slid the beam farther.

And halted on the face of a man, buried in the snow.

TWO

Horror jammed Marion's throat, blocking her air. A dead man was here? On her property?

She commanded Lily and Herc to stay and took a cautious step closer. Then another.

Honestly. She was a nurse. This wasn't her first dead body.

The admonishment pushed her feet forward until she squatted next to the man who was buried in snow from the waist down.

She scanned his black beard and caramel brown skin, pale in pallor, contusions and bruises marring his face. A split lip with dried blood. Had violence caused his injuries? Or an accident?

She reached for his neck to check his pulse.

A small noise—a squeak?—halted her movement. It came again. A meow?

Did he have a kitten with him?

She lowered her hand to a bulge beneath his black jacket. She carefully tugged the zipper pull and peeled back one edge of the leather.

Something small, ivory-colored, and round—

She sucked in a breath. A baby?

She reached to touch the infant's head, smattered with thin blond hairs.

A clamp locked around her wrist—a brown hand, cold and hard even through her jacket sleeve.

Her gaze jerked to the man's face. The very-much-not-dead man.

Eyes the color of ebony glared at her.

She shrank back. She had her hair up in a bun. Her scars were uncovered, exposed.

Herc growled and let out a deep bark, an echo of the panic coursing through Marion's veins.

Her dried mouth and pounding heartbeat screamed she should be more concerned with survival and the man who held her in a vise-like grip than the exposure of her face. She couldn't stand safely five feet away as Herc was doing.

She tugged her scarf higher over her mouth and cheeks with her left hand and forced herself to meet the stranger's gaze.

The threat in his eyes seeped away, overcome by —desperation?

"Help us." He rasped the words, his voice a deep scratch.

The baby squeaked out another small cry.

Marion's fear slid to the background at the sound. She reached her free hand to check the infant's heart rate, feel the child's temperature.

But the man groaned and grabbed at the air as if trying to locate her hand to stop her.

"I'm not going to hurt the baby. I want to help." She made contact with the infant's skin. It was warm. That was fortunate. But the baby cried louder.

Marion tugged her wrist still gripped in the man's large hand. "You have to let me go so I can help. We need to take the baby inside." Her insides coiled at the idea of inviting this probably dangerous stranger into her home at night, but she'd do what she had to for the infant.

The man's eyes slid shut. Was he slipping out of consciousness? He was likely suffering from hypothermia. Maybe more, given his injuries.

His grip didn't loosen a bit.

She firmed her voice. "The baby needs medical attention and so do you. You have to let me help the child."

His eyes opened, slowly, as if it took effort. He leveled that intense stare at her again. "I'll do it." He grunted out the words that sounded a bit like the growl Herc let loose as the man planted his hands in the snow and pushed his torso up.

At least he had to let go of Marion to accomplish the movement.

The big hand that had held her captive went to support the baby instead, cradling the child through the jacket with gentleness.

Surprise trickled through Marion's coiled insides. He looked like the toughs she'd treated in the Emergency Department after gang fights. Hardly the nurturing types.

Maybe the child was his own. Though that didn't automatically mean there'd be any affection.

She got to her feet. "Can you stand?"

He leaned forward and started to attempt the effort.

A breath pushed out audibly as he teetered over his bent knee.

She reached for his arm. If it was an arm. More like a log, thick and hard.

She did what she could to help lift him, though if he fell down again there'd be nothing she could do about it.

The man's arms matched the rest of his build. He wasn't particularly tall, though he had about five inches on her, which would make him five-ten. But every inch of him was thickly built, his muscled power obvious even through his jacket.

He took a step in the deep snow, and his weight shifted into her shoulder.

She stuck her leg out to the side to brace herself. Goodness, he was heavy.

He sucked in another breath and straightened, shifting away from her shoulder to carry his full weight. He kept the baby still tucked inside the jacket he held closed with one hand.

"Release." She signaled to Lily and Herc as they reached the dogs. "With me."

Lily trotted to Marion's side at once, but Herc stayed behind a couple of feet, staring at the stranger from a safe distance.

Normally, Marion would have prioritized Herc's comfort and helped him feel safe and less fearful. But there was nothing normal about this situation.

Though the man trudging with a limp in front of her managed to stay upright at the moment, he'd apparently already collapsed once in the snow. Who knew how long he could last now? And she still had no idea of the baby's real condition. What if the man wasn't the only one who'd been injured?

Marion hurried forward and hopped through the deep snow to get around and in front of the man. "Follow me." She used her best take-charge nurse tone. If he was going to enter her house, she'd better start earning some respect and show him she wouldn't be an easy target.

She could let him stop at the kennel since it was much closer, but she stored her First Aid kit in the house.

And the house had one other advantage. There were more rooms to hide in if this man turned out to be as dangerous as he looked.

THREE

The man collapsed onto Marion's sofa as soon she let him inside her dark house. Almost missed it as he seemed to fall more than lie down on the cushions, right on top of Marion's favorite fleece blanket.

At least he'd ended up on his back, keeping the baby safely pressed against his chest with his arm and jacket.

She inched the edges of the flashlight beam near enough to his face to see his eyes were closed again. Unconscious? If he was, she might be able to get the baby from him and do a proper assessment of the child's condition.

She released the clip that held her hair up behind her head, letting the dark brown waves fall into place, protecting and hiding.

She set the clip on the small table by the door and slipped out of her boots. She should maybe leave them on in case she needed to make a quick exit. But she didn't need to soak her rug with more of the snow that already dripped off the man's shoes. At least he'd kept his feet on the floor rather than the sofa.

She crept over to the stranger. She could probably use the

heavy metal flashlight in her hand for a weapon if he was trying to lure her close for a surprise attack.

Lily followed closely behind Marion, her tags jangling softly. Marion held her breath as she reached for the man's jacket where the baby was hidden.

"Don't try it." The man's hard warning jolted her as his eyes popped open.

Herc growled behind her. A safe distance of about six feet behind her. But at least the St. Bernard sounded and looked menacing.

The man might've thought so, too, since his gaze darted from her to Hercules and back again.

Lily pushed between Marion and the sofa and burrowed her nose into the man's jacket, clearly searching for the baby.

"Lily, leave it." Marion gripped the dog's collar and gently tugged.

Lily responded instantly, looking up at Marion as if to ask why in the world she couldn't check on the baby.

Marion was wondering the same thing. But at least the man hadn't yelled at Lily or made a move to hurt her. Hadn't even tried to push her away. That was a good sign, right?

And he was protecting a baby. Maybe he wasn't as dangerous as he looked. Despite the wounds that suggested he'd been in a fight.

She cleared her throat and kept her voice soft. "You care about the baby, don't you?" Okay, that came out more shaky than soft, but hopefully it'd help convince him she wasn't a threat. "Then let me help. I'm a nurse." Not quite, technically. But a little stretch of the truth was worth it to help a vulnerable infant.

Even weakened and injured, the man's thick arm on the baby was like a steel beam she'd never be able to move if he didn't let her.

He stared at her, his eyes as dark as midnight in the dim beam of the flashlight. Penetrating.

She dipped her head a microinch, ensuring the thick wave of hair on the left side of her face covered the ugliness.

"Okay. Go ahead."

She let out a breath, slowly so he wouldn't hear, as she reached for the baby.

"But don't go anywhere."

She paused for a moment, then noted his rough voice sounded more tired than threatening.

Marion set the flashlight on the handle's end, pointing the beam to the ceiling to cast light over the area while she kept her hands free. She extracted the infant from the jacket and brought the child close to her chest.

Lily took advantage of the moment to examine the infant herself, snuffling the soft yellow blanket wrapped around the child and ending her assessment with a gentle lick on the baby's cheek.

Tiny features puckered as the baby started to cry again. The cries weren't very strong. Could be an indication of weakness or could be normal for that infant. The baby's ivory skin was kissed with a normal hint of pink on the cheeks.

"I need to take the baby's temperature and remove the blanket for a thorough examination." She glanced at the man, catching his stare for a second before glancing away. "I'll just go to the kitchen counter." The open kitchen was behind the living room where he lay on the sofa. Shouldn't seem too threatening.

She waited a moment, then took his silence as permission. The baby, probably five to six months old, was light and easy to carry as Marion went to the kitchen. Once she pulled her enhanced First Aid kit and electric lantern from a lower cabinet, she made quick work of the examination.

The baby—a girl—seemed remarkably unharmed from

whatever trauma she'd been through tonight. At least physically. The stranger had done an amazing job protecting her from the elements and any violence he had encountered.

Admiration and relief created a warm blend in her chest, but she fought the urge to look at him over her shoulder. Her nerves already tingled with awareness that he was still watching her.

"She's doing well." The words came out quieter than she'd intended. If the man really had cared for this baby so well, didn't that suggest he wasn't a bad guy? And the infant wore a red sleeper gown smattered with cute Christmas trees and polar bears. Maybe Marion didn't have anything to be nervous about. Aside from the usual.

She touched the wave of hair to the left of her face. It hung safely over her cheek. She took a breath and tried to strengthen her tone. "All she appears to need is a diaper change. And feeding."

Marion lifted the crying baby to rest against her shoulder and walked back to the man on the sofa.

He'd managed to prop himself up to watch her over the back, but he sank down again with a wince as she approached.

"Do you have clean diapers? She's wearing a cloth one." Marion stopped in front of the sofa and looked down at the man.

Deep lines creased his brow in the shadows.

"You have cloth diapers with you, right?" Her gaze dropped from his confused expression to search for somewhere he could be carrying the needed supplies.

A dark strap she hadn't noticed before crossed his left shoulder.

"Is that a diaper bag?" She tilted her head in the direction of the strap. He hardly seemed like the type to carry a man purse. Hopefully it wasn't a rifle strap for some gun or ammo or something.

Recognition clicked in his expression, and he slowly reached for the strap. He pulled it over his head, a quiet grunt and tension at the corners of his eyes indicating the movement caused pain.

She'd have to examine him as soon as she changed the baby's diaper. That might stave off the crying long enough for her to evaluate the man's condition. He may need to go to the hospital. Which would be a real trick in this weather.

She grabbed the loose strap of the bag and tugged.

He sucked in a short, wince-laden breath as he leaned to the side, lifting off the bag he must've been partially lying on.

"Try to breathe." She hefted the bag and took it to the kitchen where she changed the baby's diaper by the light of the lantern on the counter.

The little girl's fussing quieted once the dry diaper and sleeper were in place.

Apprehension twisted Marion's belly as she returned to the stranger. She hadn't felt like this since she'd had to walk into patients' rooms at the hospital. Always wondering how they'd react to her, bracing for the worst.

She gave herself a mental shake as she rounded the end of the sofa. It was dark in here, just as it had been outside. He probably wouldn't see a thing. Wouldn't have reason to dislike her or reject her.

She pushed her shoulders back and took a breath to tell him he was next.

But her gaze fell on his closed eyes.

Had he lapsed into unconsciousness or was he only trying to rest?

She went to the armchair near the Christmas tree in the corner and nestled the baby between throw pillows there.

She spun around and walked back toward the sofa. She

stopped short. A warning flared, telling her before she looked that his eyes were open and on her face. The covered portions, hopefully.

She pushed herself forward. He could be seriously injured. No time to waste. "You're next." She squatted beside him.

His black eyebrows drew together.

"I need to examine you." She reached for his wrist.

He pulled it away. "Just take care of the baby."

She made herself meet his gaze and kept her tone firm. "I told you, she's fine right now. You did a good job keeping her warm and safe."

His gaze locked on hers, as if searching for the truth.

She didn't look away.

He let out a heavy sigh, and his lids drifted shut as he relaxed his head against her Christmas-green throw pillow.

She touched her fingers to the inside of his wrist, finding the pulse immediately.

His eyes flew open at her touch. But he didn't pull away.

"It's okay." She watched him as she counted the beats. "I need to check your vitals and examine your injuries to see how extensive they are. You may have to go to the hospital."

He jerked his arm away. "No." His eyes flashed to match his suddenly fierce tone. "No hospital."

Her own heart rate sped up as she fought the urge to pull back for safety.

This was her house, and she was the almost-nurse. She shouldn't let him intimidate her. "You may not have a choice. You could have hypothermia and judging from the beating or accident you got into, you may have internal injuries."

"I said no." He planted his hands into the cushion on either side of himself and pushed his upper body into more of a sitting position. Pain infused his eyes with the movement, but he didn't let out a sound.

She stood, putting distance between him and her. Anyone that determined not to go to the hospital when he could be severely injured had to be a criminal. Or running from the law for some reason. Explanations raced through her mind, none of them good. Or safe.

He took a breath and opened his mouth to say something she probably didn't want to hear. "I'm a cop."

FOUR

A cop? Definitely not the excuse Marion had expected to hear. Why would a cop want to avoid going to a hospital? And why would one be stranded in a snowstorm with a baby?

He didn't look like any cop she'd ever seen. And she'd seen plenty in her life.

She swallowed, working to find her voice. "If you're a cop, I'd like to see your ID."

The full lips surrounded by curly black hair tucked into a rueful smile. "No ID. I'm undercover."

A little too convenient. Though it would explain his street thug clothing. Low-fitting, loose jeans, baggy leather jacket, black beanie that matched his slightly scruffy beard.

But actually being of the criminal variety could explain the clothing even better.

She crossed her arms over her torso, the movement swishing the nylon of her jacket. "Why should I believe you?"

"I'm with the SPPD Vice Unit. I've been undercover for thirteen months in a sex trafficking ring."

She stiffened. Sex trafficking? One of the most heinous of crimes. One she'd narrowly missed.

"They brought in the baby tonight. Kidnapped from somewhere."

She shifted to the side to see the infant on the armchair. A baby? Bile surged up her throat. Was this man part of something as horrific as—

"I knew it would risk everything—my cover, all the work to break up the ring—but I couldn't let her be sold."

Sold. A human baby. A tiny helpless girl. Marion lowered her folded arms to cover her stomach as nausea swirled there.

"I tried to take her this afternoon, but I got caught."

Marion's attention switched to the man on her sofa. His split lip. The tint of bruises that darkened on his cheek and by his left eye. Had they beat him as punishment? Compassion tweaked her heart, dulling her suspicious cynicism. "How did you escape?"

"I kept them from killing me by convincing them I was only trying to steal the baby to sell her myself."

Marion's mouth tugged into a frown. Was there any truth in that claim? A flare of suspicion reignited in her brain.

"They believed me enough that they wanted to wait for the boss to find out what to do with me." His gaze stayed steadily on her as he continued, no obvious signs of lying or trying to invent a story. "They left me tied up and unconscious, they thought."

She lifted her eyebrows. "You weren't?"

"No. I managed to break free and sneak out with the baby." His hand reached toward his side as a grimace briefly crossed his face. But he lowered his arm shy of whatever injured part he'd wanted to touch—his ribs, maybe?

Her nursing instincts urged her to lean over and examine the damage. But she held herself still. Part of his story didn't make sense. "Why would you come to my place?"

"I didn't. Not intentionally." He shifted slightly, then halted the movement. Must not have relieved his discomfort. "I was going to stay in the Cities, but some of the guys saw me leave the house. They tailed me out of the city until they skidded off the road behind me. I made it farther. The snow's so deep out here, my car got stuck on the road." His gaze aimed in the direction of the baby. "I couldn't risk staying in the car with those dudes after us. Couldn't take the chance they'd find her."

So he must have headed from there on foot and ended up on her land where fatigue, cold, and perhaps his injuries caught up with him.

"If what you're saying is true, shouldn't we call the police?"

"No." A spark of urgency lit his eyes as his gaze jumped to hers. "I found out someone in the department is on the take, has a finger in the pie. I don't know how far up it goes. Can't trust anyone there." His jaw clenched, whether from determination or pain, she wasn't sure.

"I suppose that's why you don't want to go to the hospital either."

"I could be recognized. ID'd. It could get back to the trafficking ring too easily." His attention returned to the baby. "And I'm not about to leave her until she's safe anyway. I'd take her to her home tonight if I could, but I don't know where they stole her from. I don't even know her name."

Marion pressed her lips together as she mentally reviewed his story. Sounded like something out of an action movie. Or a romantic suspense novel.

But he hadn't made a move to hurt her or the baby since he'd arrived. And he could've died out in the storm while he kept the girl safe and warm. No trafficker would risk his life for a stranger's baby.

"Okay." Hopefully, she wasn't about to make a huge mistake. "No police for now. And no hospital."

His broad shoulders sagged against the cushions as his mouth relaxed its firm line.

"Unless I find you have a life-threatening injury."

His eyes narrowed slightly. But he dipped a nod. "Deal."

"Good." She leaned over him and pressed her fingers to his wrist for another check of his pulse.

His warm breaths tickled her ear as she timed the beats.

His heart rate was a bit faster than the last time, but still in the normal range.

Good thing she didn't have to take her own vitals at the moment. Her heartbeat seemed to be going crazy, tripping over itself like an adolescent puppy.

She straightened, putting some much-needed distance between herself and the man. She didn't even know his name.

"What's your name?" He asked the question as it crossed her own mind, his voice low and soft.

She moistened her dry lips. "Marion. Marion Ainsley." Her answer came out as a near-whisper as she avoided his gaze. She bent over him again, reaching for the zipper of his jacket to continue her examination.

"That's a beautiful name."

Heat flushed her face as she kept her gaze averted and unzipped the jacket in the most clinical manner she could muster. She angled her head to ensure her hair fully shrouded the left side of her face.

"I'm Eli." A slight lift in his tone tempted her curiosity, and she dared a glance.

His full lips curved into a gentle, closed smile.

She should say *nice to meet you* or a different pleasantry. The words passed through her thoughts, but she'd croak if she tried to speak, given how her throat dried to pulp under the warmth of his gaze and that sweet little smile.

She settled for a quick nod she hoped he saw as she reached to lift the hem of his black knitted sweater.

Her heart thumped against her chest. She'd had to disrobe many a patient in the ER and touched many people to treat them, take vitals, and examine. But it had never felt…intimate.

Mentally thrashing herself for her lack of professionalism, she slammed a door on her emotions—or whatever part of her was off-kilter tonight—and proceeded with efficient, clinical motions.

She left the black T-shirt he wore under the sweater alone. Given his exposure to the cold, she didn't want to remove the coverings that were keeping him warm. And she'd have no problem feeling for injuries through the thin cotton.

Her patient stayed silent as she moved her fingers across the T-shirt under his sweater.

His breathing deepened as she leaned in closer to slide her hand higher up his side. Could be a sign of increased pain from her touch.

He winced when she put light pressure on his rib.

"Sorry." She steeled herself against his discomfort as she finished the examination, repeating the assessment on his other side. Remembering his limp on the way to the house, she palpated his legs through his jeans, too.

She straightened as she finished. "Well. They sure worked you over. But the worst of the damage seems to be a couple of bruised ribs." She braved meeting his gaze. "You were lucky."

"Not lucky. God was watching out for me."

Marion never would have predicted that response. Was he serious?

His dark eyes didn't betray any sign of amusement. Neither did his expression, vertical lines bunching on his forehead as if the clarification was important to him. "So you're saying you aren't going to try to make me go to the hospital?" The lines smoothed as a smile cracked open his mouth, brightening the shadows that crossed his face.

Her heart thudded into her ribs nearly hard enough to bruise them. She turned and stepped away from the sofa, trying to catch her suddenly shallow breath. "You might have a limp for a few more days thanks to the extensive bruising on your thigh."

"They had a lot of fun kicking that for some reason."

She flinched at the image of men kicking him. Beating him.

People were horrible. As she well knew. She tried to clear her features and present her best nursing demeanor as she faced him again.

"I'll clean your split lip, but you shouldn't need stiches. Your temperature is coming up. Somehow, you seem to have avoided hypothermia."

"The burning in my hands and feet isn't too fun, but I guess it's a good thing I always tend to run hot." He slid his hand across his beard as his gaze shifted away. "Temperature-wise, I mean."

Marion grasped for the safety of her nursing persona as she battled to keep her mind from pondering the double-meaning he apparently hadn't intended. Too bad her surging pulse didn't care if it was a mistake.

She looked toward the baby and took a breath before risking another glance his way. "I do want you to remember to breathe deeply, even though the pain in your ribs will make you not want to. It's important you keep your breathing regular and deep, understood?"

Another smile seemed to play at the corners of his closed mouth. "Yes, ma'am."

Why did those two words cause butterflies to start fluttering around in her stomach?

A loud *woof* scattered the butterflies.

She hadn't paid attention to the fact Herc had stopped growling and barking at some point.

But the St. Bernard now swung to face the front door, his tail pinched against his back legs as he barked without pausing.

Marion walked toward the door, intending to look out the square window at the top.

"Don't." The man's warning halted her progress two feet from the door. "Could be them."

The traffickers?

Fear clogged her throat.

Movement outside the window caught her gaze. Someone was there.

FIVE

Marion's pulse pounded in her ears as she stood rooted in place near the door. What should she do?

A sound behind her jerked her attention to Eli.

He pushed himself to the edge of the sofa, grimacing.

"No." Not sure where the force in her voice came from, Marion leaned into the unexpected courage. She wouldn't have him hurting himself further on her account. "It's my house. I'll answer the door."

"Don't—"

"I'll look out the window first. Besides, they couldn't possibly have made it here in this weather." She raised her voice to be heard over Herc's barks. "No one could drive through that much snow."

Although someone apparently had. Unless she'd imagined the movement she'd glimpsed outside the door.

She held her breath and inched closer. Stretching up on her toes, she peered out through the corner of the window in the top third of the door.

A shadowed figure stood under the security light.

Dark jacket, pants. A beanie pulled down low.

And a sandy-colored dog that stared up at her with startling blue eyes.

Phoenix and Dagian.

Relief rushed through Marion's veins as she reached for the doorknob.

"Phoenix." Marion swung the door wide with a bigger smile than Phoenix had probably ever seen on her face.

Phoenix didn't return the friendly expression as she stepped inside with Dag. She didn't really look at Marion at all, actually. Her stare immediately landed on Eli.

The man pushed to his feet, no hint of pain on his suddenly hard features. Why was he staring so fiercely at Phoenix? Had she misjudged him?

The muscles in her abdomen tensed as Herc and Lily approached Phoenix with their tails wagging.

Phoenix didn't greet the dogs like she usually did. Her focus stayed locked on the man who looked as dangerous as when he'd first stopped Marion from touching the baby outside. Maybe he was concerned. He could think Phoenix was a threat to him and the girl.

"Eli," Marion looked from him to Phoenix, "this is my... friend." The last word barely made it out as Marion's gaze fell on the object in Phoenix's hand.

A gun.

"Phoenix?" Marion's whispered question hung in the thick air. She'd never seen Phoenix with a weapon of any kind before.

She kept the gun lowered at her side. Not aimed. But ready.

"Do you know this man?" Phoenix's deep voice apparently intended the question for Marion, though her stare didn't leave Eli.

"Um..." Marion glanced back and forth between Phoenix

and Eli, her heart rate double-timing the pace of her eyes. "Not before tonight."

Phoenix's expression showed no change, but Eli shot Marion a look that held a glint of suspicion. Like he thought she was selling him out.

She hurried to clarify. "But he's an undercover cop. He collapsed out by the kennel in the snow. With the baby he saved from traffickers." She quickly went to the armchair and scooped up the swaddled girl. Oops. The infant's closed eyes squinted open, then scrunched as she prepared to cry. She'd apparently been sleeping.

The cries started as small whines and whimpers but grew to more of a wail within seconds.

Phoenix only spared the child a split-second glance before covering Eli with her stare again. "You'd better feed her."

Marion assumed Phoenix meant she should, not Eli. Though how Phoenix knew the baby needed food was beyond Marion. "Okay. I saw some formula in the diaper bag."

She inched forward, glancing at Phoenix.

Feeling a bit like a damsel who was stupid enough to step in between the duelers in *High Noon*, she quickly passed in front of Phoenix and retreated to the kitchen.

"ID." Phoenix speared Eli with an intimidating gaze Dag seemed to mimic, both of them far more frightening now that Marion could see them from the front rather than in profile. Her vantage point behind the kitchen counter gave her a good view of Phoenix and her dog, but Eli's back was to her.

"Don't have one. Undercover." His tone was harder than when he'd spoken to Marion. But Phoenix and Dag were giving a pretty hostile impression. Hostile and daunting.

Marion's gaze drifted to the gun Phoenix still held by her leg. Would she use it? Just to protect Marion? Or was there a different reason she was carrying a gun tonight and didn't like Eli?

Questions swirled in Marion's mind as she located a can of powdered formula in the diaper bag. How well did she really know Phoenix? She mentally flipped through memories of brief conversations they'd had. Phoenix never said anything about herself. Never asked about Marion either, come to think of it. They only talked about dogs and the shelter.

"Armed."

Eli paused before answering Phoenix's implied question. "No."

Phoenix didn't relax her stance even a fraction. Or put away her gun. Clearly not taking his word for it.

"Name."

"Elijah Moore."

Phoenix continued throwing rapid-fire statements at him that seemed to be meant as questions. What department he was with. How he'd gotten to Marion's place. Where the baby had come from.

He refused to answer the last question.

"Have a seat." Phoenix's steely tone made a command out of the nicety.

Eli didn't move for a few seconds. Then he slowly lowered his big frame onto the sofa, still angling Phoenix's direction.

Marion grabbed a measuring cup from a cabinet above the opposite counter and turned back in time to see Phoenix slip the gun under her jacket where it disappeared.

Then her hand went to her pocket.

Marion froze, the scoop poised above the can in one hand while she cradled the baby in her other arm and stared. Another weapon?

A phone emerged in Phoenix's grip. She held it up, the camera lens facing Eli.

Was she taking his picture?

"Hold it." Eli barked the words just as the flash lit the darkness.

Marion blinked away the colored spots in her vision.

"What are you going to do with that?" Eli threw the question at Phoenix, his voice tense.

"Check your story."

"You can't do that. You'll blow my cover."

Phoenix stared at him.

"I know it's in jeopardy already." The hard edge of Eli's tone softened as he apparently felt the need to explain under her unrelenting gaze. "But no one can know where I am or that I have the baby here. Her life depends on it."

And so did Eli's.

"I'll be discreet."

"How do I know I can trust you? Who are you?"

"Either I check into you myself, or I can take you to the police right now."

Marion's eyes widened till she thought they might pop out of her head. Where did Phoenix get the guts to say that to a hulking man like Eli? The woman was probably two inches taller than Marion and in terrific shape, but still.

"And just how do you think you'd manage that?" Eli was calling Phoenix's bluff.

Marion held her breath.

Phoenix didn't blink. "Could use this." She pressed her fingers to the spot under her jacket where she'd stashed the gun. "But I won't have to."

The woman was astonishing. No fear or defiance or anger showed on Phoenix's face. Shadows hid her golden skin and the eyes Marion knew to be dark blue. And almost always inscrutable.

"Fine." Eli's answer allowed air to reenter Marion's lungs.

"You're holding the cards, and I have nothing to hide. From the right people."

Phoenix abruptly moved, passed by the darkened Christmas tree in the corner, and stopped at the edge of the kitchen. She spun away so she stood perpendicular to Marion while facing the back of the sofa where Eli sat, his head twisted toward Phoenix. Dag sat next to Phoenix's leg.

A louder cry from the baby reminded Marion she was supposed to be mixing formula. She added the powder to the bottle and went to the sink.

"I'll get the generator going for the house." Phoenix watched Eli as she spoke with a slightly lowered tone, but Marion assumed the information was meant for her.

Relief eased some of the tension in Marion's muscles as she added warm water to the bottle. She'd wondered how she was going to leave the baby and stranger alone in her house to go start the generator. "Thank you." She pulled the bottle out from under the water stream and turned off the faucet.

"I'm going to stick around tonight." Phoenix still eyed Eli. "I'll check on the dogs and watch for visitors."

Visitors. Marion had trouble swallowing. "I didn't think anyone could get through in this weather. Unless they got stranded like..." Her gaze drifted to Eli. But Phoenix had made it through somehow. Did that mean the traffickers could, too?

"I had to stop two miles away and came in on snowshoes. Pulled Dag in a sled."

Marion blinked at Phoenix's profile. How did the woman even know to do all that? And she'd gone to such lengths to get there to check on the dogs. "Thank you." Gratitude welled up in Marion's chest.

"Doubtful they'll come tonight." Phoenix angled half toward Marion, her gaze caught in shadow. "The wind might pick up tomorrow, which could make access easier by blowing the snow clear in places. I'll check on the house frequently tonight." Phoenix turned her head directly toward Marion, her dark blue eyes steady, expression unreadable. "Call or text me for any reason." She looked in Eli's direction. "If he checks out, we'll prep for hostiles tomorrow."

Marion had opened her mouth to say Phoenix didn't have to stay all night, to ask if she wanted to sleep in the guest room, to offer coffee, food, or hot chocolate.

But the word *hostiles* pinched her throat, and Phoenix slipped out of the house within seconds, Dag's sandy tail the last to disappear through the front door.

"Who was that?" Eli's rough voice curbed Marion's fear, stoking her confusion and wonder.

She stared at the door where Phoenix had come and gone. "I thought I knew."

SIX

A noise reached into Marion's sleep. Her dreaming mind explained the sound as Lily whining.

The noise grew louder. Stranger.

Marion slowly opened her eyes.

The baby. Her soft, fussy cries filtered through the room with the same hope carried by the light that pushed through the bedroom window curtains. The light of day had arrived, and the baby was healthy, crying as she should to make her needs known.

Marion slipped her legs out from under the comforter, reaching over to pet Lily, who had slept beside Marion on the bed, as usual.

Marion shoved her feet into slippers, and Lily hopped off the bed to the floor.

Hercules rose from the dog bed in the corner and yawned as he stretched.

The baby's crying grew a little stronger.

"It's okay, baby girl. I'm coming." It felt wrong not to be able to call the girl by her name. But, hopefully, she wouldn't be nameless for long.

Eli had told Marion last night that he intended to find out who she was and where she'd come from.

"I'll get her home. Whatever it takes."

The determination in his gaze when he'd said those words filled Marion's memory as she shuffled over to the dresser drawer she'd lined with blankets to create a cozy bed for the infant. The tiny girl looked fine, so Marion took a moment to go to her two windows and open the curtains covering them. More light illuminated the bedroom, despite the heavy shower of snowflakes that continued to fall outside. They were giant flakes now, still accumulating fast.

The ground beneath the second-story window was covered in multiple feet of cottony white fluff. A winter wonderland. Perfect weather for Christmas Eve.

If she didn't have a fugitive man and baby stranded at her house.

The little one's fussing pulled Marion from the window. She went to her bedroom door first and pulled away the chair she'd wedged under the doorknob last night before going to bed. Eli probably wasn't a bad man, since he'd risked his life for the baby. But she wouldn't have been able to sleep a wink if she hadn't had some barrier between her and the stranger in her house.

Swinging the door open so she could get through easier with the baby, she returned to the dresser where Herc was gently snuffling the tiny visitor. Marion picked up the girl and brought her close, rocking and cooing over her. Marion peeled back the yellow blanket to feel the diaper. The infant's crying dissipated, her scrunched features smoothing.

"You're a natural."

Marion's heart jumped into her throat at the male voice.

Eli stood in the doorway, his thick shoulder leaned against the frame as he watched her.

She instinctively turned her head more to the left, fighting the urge to reach for her hair to be sure it was in place. It hung loose. The long hair should be covering the scar.

But she couldn't do anything about the fact she was only in her pajamas. The fleece pants and long-sleeve top covered everything, but it still felt...vulnerable.

"Sorry. I didn't mean to startle you."

Herc stayed by Marion, eyeing Eli, but Lily trotted to greet him. He stroked her head with a big hand. "I heard the baby crying and wanted to check on her." Eli's voice was rougher and deeper in the morning, a sound that rippled through her all the way to her toes. "You look nice holding her."

Her gaze jumped to his as warmth flooded her chest.

His mouth curved in a soft smile. He didn't look so dangerous this morning. In fact, he looked undeniably handsome. Not like an actor or model, but his strong features and broad face gave him a masculine presence that made her nervous and drew her to him at the same time.

His beanie was no longer in sight, freeing his black hair to shape his head—a shorter version of the beard that was just long enough to make her fingers want to explore the curls. His brown complexion looked healthier and more vibrant.

But his eyes were what stopped her, made her unable to look away. They appeared to be more of a shade of mahogany in the light from the windows.

And a look she couldn't interpret lit the orbs. Though it seemed familiar. Like...

Her breath caught. Was that the look the heroes in the Christmas romances she'd been watching had in their eyes? The way they looked at the heroine the first time they met, and they'd watch her...with admiration and something more.

It couldn't be. But Marion's heartbeat double-timed anyway, somehow able to keep pumping though she couldn't breathe.

He straightened and let his gaze flit away as he cleared his throat.

She'd probably made him uncomfortable with her staring and silence. Good grief. She'd been watching way too many romances lately. Of course he wasn't interested in her. Even though he must not have seen the scar last night.

"Do you have any kids?"

His question was surprising enough to make her risk a quick glance in his direction as embarrassment reached her face in a rush of heat. "No. Never married." She stifled an eyeroll as soon as the words left her mouth. Honestly. Now she sounded ridiculously old-fashioned, too.

"You must have a boyfriend."

She shook her head.

"I just thought...because you're so good with babies." He rubbed the back of his neck with his hand. Maybe she wasn't the only one who felt awkward. Probably thanks to her. She'd stared at the poor man like a desperate, googly-eyed female.

She shrugged. "I did a rotation in the neonatal intensive care unit."

"That's right." He smiled. A bigger smile that made her pulse trip over itself. "You're a nurse."

She hid a wince. Never had been much of a liar. Her mom had proven that only led to disaster. "I'm not technically a nurse."

"Oh?" His thick, curved eyebrows lifted, but his tone didn't hold any judgment.

"I didn't quite finish the program."

"Why was that? You seem good at it."

The reactions she'd never forget flashed in her memory. The horrified expressions on the faces of patients' family members when she was supposed to give them updates. The mothers who whisked their babies out of her arms with wide eyes and later asked for a different nurse. The patient—the little boy—who'd cried in his hospital bed and screamed she was a monster when she'd tried to take his vitals.

Marion cleared her throat and shifted the baby higher, against her shoulder. "It wasn't a good fit."

She walked toward the door, but Eli didn't move out of her way.

She let her gaze find his.

He looked at her, his brow furrowed above his dark eyes.

Did he know what she meant? Her insides clenched. He hadn't seen the scar, had he? It had been so dark last night when her hair was away from—

"Their loss. You did a great job patching me up."

The reference brought her attention to the first things a good nurse should have assessed. The bruises on his cheeks above his beard that were more obvious than they were last night. His swollen lip split by the cut. Though it didn't look like it had bled anymore after she'd cleaned it. She could imagine his rib pain was still significant, as well.

"I look worse than I feel." He gave her a cute smile that curled her innards again.

The baby waved her little hands in the air as she let out a short cry.

Marion swallowed. "I changed her diaper about an hour ago. I think she's hungry."

"Can I help?" Eli stepped into the hallway, letting Marion and the dogs pass by as he stood to the side. "I could make her breakfast." That adorable eager smile—a little boy sweetness on a tough-guy's face—was going to be Marion's undoing.

Even Herc seemed to be falling under Eli's charm. The hulking St. Bernard shoved between Marion and Eli to jog ahead without a speck of fear.

A small smile found her own lips at Herc's relaxed behavior. He must have decided Eli was okay, too. She glanced at the man. "I think I can do breakfast for her and you."

She turned away before he could respond and started up the hallway with Lily and the baby. Trying not to imagine he watched her with that hero's look.

And, of course, he wouldn't. She wore unflattering but thoroughly comfortable pajamas and hadn't even been able to run a brush through her hair, let alone change or shower.

With those embarrassing truths firmly in hand, Marion didn't look back at Eli as they reached the first floor, and she went to the kitchen where she flicked the light switch.

Thanks to the generator Phoenix had hooked up last night, the light fixture in the kitchen lit, as would the lamps in the living room if she flipped the switch.

Eli caught up with Marion and Lily at the kitchen counter. Herc had peeled off somewhere. Probably to the back door where she usually let him outside first thing.

Movement by the Christmas tree in the living room caught Marion's gaze.

Eli stepped partially in front of her as a figure emerged from the shadows. With a smaller figure beside her.

Phoenix and Dagian.

Marion started to breathe again.

Until Phoenix spoke. "We have trouble."

SEVEN

Marion's pulse raced as she waited for Phoenix to elaborate. Which could sometimes be a long wait.

"The forecasters are more certain blizzard winds will begin this afternoon." At least Phoenix was offering information this time. Though Marion didn't quite see the problem.

"The wind could clear some areas and build deeper drifts in others. Could create paths, easier access to reach your property and access the kennel and house." Phoenix apparently spoke to Marion, but her gaze seemed to encompass Eli, as well.

Especially since Eli still stood close. Very close.

His warmth permeated Marion's pajamas. And her senses.

The baby knocked her little hands into Marion's chest and cried. Perfect timing.

"The roads, however, are still nearly impassable for most people right now." Phoenix continued as if unaware of Marion's wild romantic imaginings. "When the wind picks up, they'll still be difficult to navigate due to drifting."

Marion stepped away to busy herself with prepping formula before she got even more carried away.

Lily greeted Phoenix by sniffing her black jeans and was rewarded with some ear scratches.

"Plows won't make it out this way for a while." Phoenix stepped to the far end of the sofa and bent to pick something up. She hefted a gray case that looked like an oversized, hard-sided briefcase.

She plunked the case on the coffee table and touched it just above the handle.

Beeps sounded. Was she typing in a code on a pad?

Marion scooped out formula from the can as she watched Phoenix.

Eli seemed just as mesmerized by the curiosity that was Phoenix. Or maybe he was suspicious. His posture did seem rigid, and his stare stayed on Phoenix. As if preparing for what she might pull from the case.

"You checked out." Phoenix sent him a slow, steady glance as she flipped open the lid.

Was that...? Marion eyed the contents. Thanks to the coffee table being so low, she could see inside better than she wanted to.

Weapons. A whole arsenal of guns in different sizes and shapes. A shiver tracked down Marion's arms. Where had Phoenix gotten those? Why would she have them? And did she really think they needed such things now? Here, at Marion's home?

The baby turned her head into Marion's chest, a reminder she was hungry. Marion finished dumping formula into the bottle and added warm water at the faucet.

She glanced toward the living room as she shook the bottle to mix the contents.

Eli had moved closer to Phoenix and stood behind the sofa where he could probably better see the weapons. "Do you have permits for these?"

"You can pick two or three to borrow." Phoenix ignored

his question as she reached in the case and drew out a small handgun. Or pistol. Marion couldn't tell the difference. If there was a difference.

Phoenix marched around the sofa toward Marion with the gun in her hand.

Marion's heart rate kicked up as Phoenix grew closer, and the beats stopped altogether when she rounded the counter. "You'll use this one."

Marion stepped back. She gripped the bottle tighter and tipped it to the baby's mouth. "No, thanks." She focused on making sure the girl sucked normally.

"You're likely to need it."

Marion closed her eyes. Exactly what her nerves didn't need to hear. But what if Phoenix was right? She clearly knew what she was doing.

Marion looked up and met Phoenix's dark blue eyes. "I don't know how to use it."

"You will by nightfall." The confidence in Phoenix's steady gaze and her assured tone gave Marion some comfort even though her words were slightly terrifying.

The woman walked back to Eli, drawing Marion's attention to the two guns—a pistol and a longer-barreled gun—in his hand. He set two boxes on the table. Ammunition?

Marion tried to swallow, but all traces of saliva seemed to soak into the sandpaper dryness of her throat.

"We need to strategize." Phoenix looked at Eli, the length of the coffee table between them. "You know the men involved. Will they come for the child?"

"Yes." He answered without hesitation. "A baby means big money to them."

Disgust loosened some of the fear caking Marion's throat. How could anyone think of a baby that way?

"We must leave." Phoenix's statement screeched Marion's thoughts to a halt.

Leave?

"How?" Eli set the weapons he'd chosen on the coffee table.

"Same way I got in. Marion has snowshoes, as well."

"You just said the roads are impassable." Eli crossed his arms over his broad chest.

Phoenix widened her stance, apparently undaunted by the picture of strength before her. "Impassable for most people. Not for me. I have chains on my tires and equipment to dig out my SUV if I need to."

"I'm not risking the baby out there again." Intensity edged Eli's tone. "It was necessary before, but right now she's safer here. At least until the storm lets up."

The tension emanating between Eli and Phoenix was palpable even from the kitchen. Phoenix's voice and expression were as dispassionate as ever, but Eli's stiff posture and hardening tone said he felt challenged. And would refuse to yield.

Marion's stomach twisted, her nerves standing on edge like they always did at any hint of conflict. She should interrupt before things got more heated. "I couldn't leave anyway."

Both sets of eyes targeted her.

She swallowed, choosing to meet Phoenix's more familiar gaze. "The dogs. I can't leave them." She glanced at Eli. "But you two should go with the baby. If you think that's best."

Eli shook his head. "That confirms it." He faced Phoenix again. "We can't leave Marion alone."

Warmth flooded Marion's torso and overflowed to her limbs, all the way to her fingertips on the baby bottle. Did he care about her?

"I'll need to take the baby." Phoenix's statement doused the rare moment of hope without ceremony. Eli wasn't going to like that idea.

"Absolutely not." His voice sharpened. "It's too dangerous."

"Not at all." Phoenix didn't change her tone or stance as she met Eli's resistance with her usual matter-of-fact demeanor. "I'm equipped for search and rescue missions at all times. I have survival gear that will ensure the baby's safety in any conditions we encounter."

"No offense, but I don't know you." Eli lowered his arms, softening his stance. But his resolve seemed unshakable. "The baby stays with me."

Marion's clenched stomach churned, adding nausea to the nervous mix. This much hostility before breakfast was a bad idea. "We should eat." The words slipped out before she gave them much thought.

But the gazes that aimed at her weren't hostile. In fact, Eli's mouth curved slightly in the beginning of a smile.

"I mean, Eli needs to eat. His body experienced a lot of trauma yesterday. Nutrition is important." She looked away, studying the baby as she sucked the last of the formula from the bottle. "And once I finish feeding the baby, I have to feed the dogs and check the runs for snow in case any blew in." The unnecessary detail gave her a reason to keep talking and hopefully time for Phoenix and Eli to stop arguing. Although their argument was probably the least heated Marion had ever seen.

"I already did."

Marion blinked at Phoenix. "The dogs?"

Phoenix gave a short nod.

"Thank you. I need to take poor Lily and Hercules out, though. They're not used to waiting this long in the morning to go."

As if on cue, Herc jogged out from the short hallway that led to the back door and looked at Marion with a whine.

Phoenix closed the case of weapons and picked it up. "I'll take them. Then I'll exercise the other dogs and keep watch."

"You're staying?"

Phoenix met Marion's scrutiny across the counter and space between them. "For now. No one's likely to make it through until this afternoon or evening."

Meaning the traffickers. Marion's throat started to close. "Since the snow's so deep, you can use the training room and the flirt toy for Peppy and Oliver." She didn't know how she managed to put those thoughts together and sound so normal when her insides were quaking. "Thanks for your help. I'll come out soon."

Phoenix paused, then looked at Eli and Marion with a thoroughly unreadable expression. Did Phoenix sense something between them? The current of attraction Marion felt even with a counter and several feet between them? Or maybe Phoenix just thought Marion was a mess and should shower and change.

Phoenix turned and left with Dag before Marion could decipher the hidden message. If there was one.

Silence hovered in the house. For a second.

"So who exactly is she?" Eli angled toward Marion, his thick eyebrows more prominent when they were scrunched in puzzlement.

Marion hadn't known how to answer that question last night. She still wasn't sure she had an adequate answer now that she was seeing sides to Phoenix she'd never known existed.

"Is she FBI?" Eli walked toward the counter from the living room side.

Never thought of that. "I don't think so. She volunteers at Forever Home, helping care for the dogs."

"But where'd she come from? What does she do?" He

stopped at the counter and pushed his fingers into his jeans pockets.

"I don't know. She first came about a year ago, in January."

"After you met her somewhere?"

"No." Marion knew she must be the one who looked perplexed now. But it had always surprised her. "She just showed up out of nowhere." Literally, it seemed, since Marion hadn't seen her standing by a dog run Marion was cleaning until the woman spoke. "She seemed almost too good to be true." Actually, at first she'd been unnerving. Quiet with a stare that seemed to see and know everything but give nothing away.

Marion kept that extra information to herself. It would be disloyal to make Phoenix appear suspicious. "She's very interested in dog training. She said she wanted to learn my training methods."

"Is there something special about your training methods?"

"Not particularly. I use force-free, pain-free techniques with great results."

A small smile played on Eli's lips, and his eyes softened. "Why does that not surprise me?"

A flutter traveled from her belly up into her chest under his warm gaze. She glanced away, flitting her focus to the dark tree, a gloomy specter without the cheery lights that would require more electricity than the generator was powering.

"I see you have a lot of presents under your tree. Is your family coming for Christmas?"

She looked at the small packages piled on the skirt under the pine. Each one was wrapped in colorful Christmas paper—gifts for the shelter dogs and Lily and Hercules. "No."

"Are you going to them then? I hope I'm not interfering with any family traditions being here."

"You're not." Her throat tightened. "Are you spending Christmas with family?" She kept her gaze away from him as she launched the counter question.

"I wish. Doesn't work with my cover." A wistfulness in his tone brought her attention to his face. "I missed last Christmas, too."

Her chest pinched a little at the sadness that pulled down the corners of his mouth. She looked away from the expression that was probably a reflection of her own. "That's too bad. It's great to be with family at Christmas." At least that was what all the Christmas movies and songs claimed. It had never been good to be with her mom any time of year.

But she'd better change topic before he asked her anything more on the subject.

She set the now-empty bottle on the counter and used a soft dishcloth to dab up the formula that had seeped onto the baby's tiny lips. "Do you like eggs?" She lifted her gaze to find Eli, but he wasn't in the living room anymore.

"Sure do."

Her heart jumped at his voice so near her shoulder. Amazing she hadn't felt the heat from his closeness that she was overwhelmingly aware of now.

She tried to swallow, then abandoned the effort since it seemed so difficult at the moment. "I'll scramble some." She turned away and reached for the refrigerator door.

"Can I hold the baby while you do that? Or I can scramble the eggs. Believe it or not, I'm a decent cook." The humor in his voice beckoned her like the playful yip of a puppy.

Her gaze drifted up and somehow fell into his eyes, dark pools of mahogany comfort that made her want to stay forever.

Those eyes crinkled at the corners. "Marion?"

Her name on his lips broke the spell even as it sent a shiver up her arms.

Honestly. What was she doing staring at him like that? He was going to think she was crazy. "The baby." Heat crawled toward her cheeks. "You can take the baby." The small infant's weight had grown surprisingly heavy in Marion's arms holding her so long.

"I was hoping that's what you'd say." He stepped closer.

Awareness skittered through Marion, prickling every sense she owned except the rational common sense she could really use right about now.

He held out his big hands toward the baby. "Come here, sweetheart."

Sweetheart. Her insides nearly melted at the tenderness in his voice. What would it be like to hear him say that to her?

Marion somehow managed to have the wherewithal to move the baby toward Eli, but he'd already come most of the way.

His hands brushed against her arms as he scooped up the infant.

At least Marion assumed he was doing that. She was too focused on his closeness, the sparks and heat flooding her all at once with his head so close to hers.

That head lifted, and his dark eyes locked on hers.

Did she imagine it, or did his breathing slow and deepen?

The baby gurgled between them.

Eli smiled, gently, almost like an acknowledgement they'd shared something that was being interrupted. That he didn't want to end.

Or maybe that she was blowing way out of proportion with her Christmas-romance-fueled imagination.

He moved away with the baby, leaving her to wonder if she'd dreamt the whole thing.

Her hand jerked to the hair that should be shielding her

scar. It was there. Hiding everything. She breathed again. But her pulse didn't slow. He'd been so close he could've seen.

She should be worried about the danger of violent men about to descend on her home. But nothing scared her more in that moment than the look she would see on his face if he ever really saw her.

EIGHT

Marion watched Eli as much as she dared while his eggs cooked. The sight of the burly undercover cop cradling a tiny baby in his strong arms at the breakfast table in the kitchen had to be the most endearing thing she'd ever seen.

He grinned down at the little girl and gently tapped her nose with his finger.

She bobbed her fists in response.

Marion couldn't see the baby's face from the stove, but she guessed Eli was earning some smiles. Charmer.

A smile found Marion's face, too, as she turned back to check the eggs.

She glanced over her shoulder again, and her gaze hit Eli's. A flutter tickled in her belly. Had he seen her watching him?

She covered with what she hoped was a casual attempt at conversation. "Seems like you know babies. Do you have kids?"

"No. I always wanted a family, though." He gave the little girl in his arms a wistful smile. "Thought I'd have a bunch of kids, but God hasn't sent me the right woman yet."

Marion's eyebrows went up at the mention of God—so strange coming from a tough guy like Eli. But his love of children explained a lot. "Is that why you risked your life for the baby?"

"That was easy. I couldn't let them..." His mouth reversed to a frown as he looked at the infant, then up at Marion. "It's hard to do the assignment I've been on, patiently working my way to the top. I have to remind myself every day that this is the way we can save them all. And prevent more from being taken." His jaw shifted under his beard. "But when they brought her, this little baby, right to the house where I was." He shook his head, his eyes glimmering with what looked like moisture. "I couldn't let them destroy her."

A lump formed in Marion's throat as tears blurred her own eyes. She'd never seen a man show any tender emotion. Not compassion and definitely never tears. "Some men could have."

His gaze found hers, lines crossing his brow. "Men you've known?"

The question hung between them, the answer too dark and deep for her to speak.

A sizzle behind her drew her attention. She spun away to finish scrambling the eggs. She made quick work of them in the silence, then plated the yellow feast and carried it to him at the table.

"I'm a man of God, Marion." Eli's unexpected statement grabbed her gaze as she set the plate in front of him. "God made this little girl in His image. She's precious. God wants me to do everything I can to keep her, and others like her, from evil."

Marion switched her focus from Eli to the baby he said was precious. The baby he'd risk his own life to save. Her tiny features were so perfect, from her button nose to the soft, unblemished milky skin. No scars. Maybe for a girl so perfect, a man would be willing to die. "She is beautiful."

Silence met Marion's soft words. She'd thought Eli would heartily agree.

Maybe he thought it was so obvious he didn't need to say anything. She glanced at him as she straightened.

His dark brown eyes watched her intently.

Panic surged up her throat. Could he see the scar?

"So are you, Marion."

The statement didn't make sense at first as it crashed headlong into the wave of fear.

Wait. Had he just said she was beautiful?

Her hand went to the long hair that should be covering the left side of her face. She tried to make the move look natural as she smoothed her fingers down the locks. Her shield was still in place.

She breathed again, but only for a second before she remembered what Eli had said.

His gaze tracked the movement of her hand as she pulled it away from her hair. She shouldn't have drawn attention to that side of her face. To the horrific scar that would shatter any illusion he might have that she was beautiful.

"Everything God makes is beautiful."

He'd said it again. Beautiful. About her.

But God hadn't made her scar. Her mom's boyfriend had. Maybe the man who was Marion's father. She'd never know. But she knew the destruction of the left side of her face wasn't beautiful. And neither was she.

Reality clicked into place as she realized what Eli had actually meant. He didn't mean to say he thought she was beautiful, not in a romantic way. He apparently thought everything was beautiful.

Did that include evil men who trafficked children? Or people who abused dogs and—

Never mind.

Marion needed to get off this romantic fantasy train and back to reality before she made even more of a fool of herself. "Enjoy your breakfast. I need to help Phoenix with the dogs."

She practically dashed out the door, hopefully in time to save her heart.

———

"Just wait here for a little bit." Marion opened the door that connected the kennel section of the building to the training room and slipped through before Lily and Herc could follow her. "I'll be right back."

Phoenix had let Lily and Herc wander around the kennel area as Marion often did while she worked with dogs in the training area.

The woman with the long blond braid down her back now played with Oliver at the far end of the long room that was partitioned into two halves.

Marion passed through the home section, where she'd set up sofas, a dining table, and dog crates. The space simulated a typical home environment to acclimate dogs before they were hopefully adopted.

She stepped over the long barrier that split the room into sections and watched Phoenix walk around, jerking the flirt toy back and forth to lure the hound mix.

Somehow, Dagian held a down stay in the far corner, calmly watching the toy that made most dogs lose their minds. He was the steadiest dog Marion had ever known. As unique and controlled as his owner.

Oliver let out a bark as he leaped for the ferret-like plush toy on the end of a line attached to the pole Phoenix held in her hand.

"Looks like he's been going at it hard." Marion grinned at

the sight of the long tongue hanging from Oliver's mouth and the crazed look in his eyes as he tried to pounce on the toy.

"Time for a water break." Phoenix let Oliver catch the toy in his mouth.

Marion moved toward Phoenix now that she stood in one place. "The snow's still coming down hard."

Phoenix closed the distance between herself and Oliver. "Drop."

Oliver instantly released the toy from his mouth and sat in front of her for a treat.

Loving pride warmed Marion's chest. A lot of work had gone into getting that boy to give up a toy on command.

He jogged to the water dish while Phoenix hung the flirt toy on a high hook on the wall, then turned to Marion.

Phoenix stood there silently. Waiting. As if she knew Marion had more to say.

"Do you really think the danger from…whoever might come is so bad that you should risk yourself and the baby in this weather?

"Yes." Pheonix's answer came immediately, her gaze unflappable.

Marion's ribs squeezed a bit closer together. So much for hoping Phoenix would calm her fears. Maybe tell her traffickers weren't coming to her house or that nothing bad would happen even if they did. That this was all just a scary movie with a happily-ever-after ending. Maybe a romantic one.

Marion caught her bottom lip with her teeth. None of that was true, and she knew it. A sense of resolve solidified in her mind. She'd have to say what she had hoped she wouldn't have to. "Then you and Eli should go, take the baby away from here together. He'd probably agree to it if he went along."

"No."

Marion blinked. She'd expected Phoenix to agree, since it had been her idea to leave. "But the baby needs to go. She can't fall into the hands of traffickers." Marion's stomach churned at the thought. "We can't let that happen to her."

Phoenix's blue eyes penetrated Marion's, though her expression didn't seem to change. "I'm taking the child."

Marion tilted her head. She must be missing something. "But you just said…"

"Moore needs to trust me to do it alone."

"Oh. Because he won't let you take her otherwise?"

"Because he needs to stay with you."

Marion's heart twisted, whether because she wanted him to stay or because she wanted him to save the baby, she couldn't say for sure. "It's okay for you both to go. I won't be responsible for you leaving the baby here in danger for my sake." She glanced at Oliver, who had collapsed in a happily exhausted heap with his long ear dangling into the water bowl. "But I can't leave the dogs."

"No, you can't."

Relief lessened the tightness in Marion's chest a tad. At least Phoenix understood her responsibility to the dogs.

"And I won't leave you unprotected."

Marion ran her tongue over her lips. "But how will you get Eli to let you take the baby alone?"

"You might be accomplishing that for me."

What in the world did Phoenix mean by that? Marion opened her mouth to ask—

"The extra time here will be useful." Phoenix continued before Marion could question her. "If the roads become easier to navigate later when the strong winds come, I'll be able to ensure you and Moore are prepared for the intruders."

A shiver passed through Marion at the reminder. She reached for the courage to ask what she was afraid to. "What will they do? If they come..." There didn't seem to be an *if* in Phoenix's plans, but Marion had to hope they might never find Eli and the baby there. That they'd never come at all.

"They'll want to take you with them."

Trepidation seized her chest, crushing her ribs in a vise. Clutching fear gripped her like it used to. Her old childhood companion.

"I'll do everything I can to help you survive." Phoenix's firm voice came from much closer, as if she stood near Marion's elbow.

But Marion barely heard her. Last night, she'd been afraid Christmas morning would be lonely. Now she only hoped she'd be alive to see it.

Hours later, the same dread and anxiety had mixed a nauseating blend in her stomach and kept a fist clenched around every muscle she had. The planning meeting Phoenix held before lunch hadn't helped.

Marion had completely lost her appetite by the time Phoenix and Eli were through plotting a defense strategy, as they called it, for the imminent invasion.

It seemed a fine plan under the circumstances, as far as Marion could tell, but nothing could calm the fear making itself at home in her unsettled system. She tried to focus on breathing normally as she went from kennel to kennel, giving the dogs kibble for lunch and refreshing their water supply.

A loud grinding sound made Marion start.

Calm down. She glanced at Phoenix and the electric screwdriver she was using to secure boards across the front door. She'd wedged a small piece of wood under the door, as well, but Marion was learning Phoenix left nothing to chance. The barricade would be very secure before she was done.

Marion forced a swallow down her throat. She appreciated the effort, of course, to make sure the dogs were safe. The front and side doors would be barricaded. The back door alone would be usable but locked with the assumption the traffickers would only enter the kennel if they found an easy-to-open door on their way to the house. Both Phoenix and Eli thought the traffickers would most likely go to the house first to look for the baby or other people there.

Marion was glad the dogs would likely be left alone, and that was the point in staying away from them herself unless Eli saw anyone enter the kennel.

But it wasn't entirely comforting to have confirmation that the men would most want to get into her house. Where she and Eli would be. Eli could probably protect her, though. He seemed to know what he was doing. And he was certainly strong—

A low growl jerked Marion's gaze toward Phoenix.

Dagian's tan body went rigid as he growled again, his upright ears aimed with his stare at something outside the front door.

Hercules woofed and jogged to Dag's side.

Lily looked up at Marion with curiosity in her eyes.

"Phoenix?"

The woman held up a hand like a stop signal.

A faint rumbling sound permeated the walls. What—

Phoenix suddenly broke into a jog toward the side door at the end of the building closest to the house. Dag easily matched her pace, and Hercules loped after them.

Lily stayed at Marion's side as she quickly snatched two leashes off a hook on the wall. She clipped one to Lily's harness, then trotted after Phoenix.

The woman slipped through the door with Dag, leaving a barking Hercules inside.

Marion's hand trembled as she fastened Herc's leash. She sucked in a breath and opened the door.

She carefully stuck her head outside.

Phoenix stood at the corner of the building and looked

toward the front yard. Her gun was gripped in the hand at her side.

"With me." Marion whispered the command to Lily and Herc as she stepped out and headed toward Phoenix.

Cold snow fell into her boots as she trudged forward, and Lily had to leap to break through the two feet of white fluff. More flakes dampened Marion's cheeks and hair.

The rumbling grew louder.

But it couldn't be anyone coming. Not yet. How could they in this snow? Maybe it was a plow on the roads nearby.

Marion stopped beside Phoenix. "What is it?"

The answer appeared on the white horizon. A dark, round shape crested the low hill in the distance. Then another one to the right of the first. Then one more.

The shapes grew bigger and more definable as they moved down the hill.

Heads. Attached to darkly clothed bodies.

Three people on snowmobiles. Coming closer.

NINE

One of the snowmobiles stopped, but the other two kept coming as fear froze Marion in place.

"How—"

"Backcountry snowmobiles." No irritation or fear laced Phoenix's stoic statement.

"Do you think it's them?"

"Go to the house." Phoenix's command was her answer. "Stay with the baby. Tell Moore to protect you both at the house."

Panic quaked through Marion, but her feet didn't move.

The traffickers had come.

A touch through her jacket sleeve brought Marion's attention to blue eyes.

Phoenix's penetrating gaze cut through the panic. "Run. Now." Her sharp tone jolted Marion into action.

She took off for the house, Lily and Herc bounding through the deep snow with her.

Fire burned Marion's lungs as she hit the front door and nearly fell inside.

"What's—" Eli stood from the sofa, the baby sleeping in his arms.

"They're here." Marion choked out the words as she panted for breath. "Snowmobiles."

Eli's features settled into a mask of intensity and...protectiveness? He closed the distance between them, and his hand went to touch her shoulder. "Are you okay?"

No, she wasn't. But she'd be a lot worse if those monsters got into the house. To the baby. To her.

She mustered a nod. "Phoenix said you should stay here with the baby and..." *Me.* She let the word go unsaid. It would be the first time in her life someone wanted to protect her, to care for her in any way. She wasn't about to start believing it could be true now. Not with someone like Eli who could have any woman much more desirable than—

"Marion?"

She yanked her gaze up to his face. Must have missed what he'd said. Probably couldn't hear it thanks to the adrenaline-laced blood rushing in her ears. "Sorry."

"I need you to take the baby. And let's put the dogs somewhere safe." His tone was calm, but serious. In control.

Marion extended her arms to take the infant as Eli handed her over.

He immediately marched to the table and grabbed the weapons he'd borrowed from Phoenix.

Marion sent Lily and Herc to the study and closed the door. Herc immediately started barking, probably alarmed by her odd behavior and obvious apprehension.

The baby made a small sound and turned her head into Marion's chest. Her tiny eyelids remained shut.

Marion's heart squeezed. If only this little one could sleep through the whole thing. Not be touched by any more danger.

"Two are coming closer." Eli stood by the front window to

the left of the door, the longer gun in his hand and the smaller one protruding from the waistband behind his back. "Wait. They peeled off, split up." He glanced over his shoulder at her. "Probably trying to get out of sight as they go around the building." He faced her and met her gaze. "It'll be okay."

Could he see that her pulse was running at triple speed, and she was forgetting to breathe?

"If your friend Phoenix is half as competent as she acts like she is, we'll be able to handle two or three of these guys between the both of us." His mouth curved into a half-smile. "And maybe these are just some dudes out for a crazy joy ride in dangerous conditions. They might not have anything to do with me and the baby."

Air slowly seeped back into Marion's lungs under the effect of his soothing tone. His cute smile. His attempt to calm her. As if he cared.

"But maybe go behind the sofa, just in case." He gave her a fuller smile now, and his dark eyes even twinkled.

The corner of her mouth twitched like it wanted to respond in kind but couldn't manage the effort on so little oxygen. She gave him a nod and went around the sofa where she kneeled on the rug, cradling the baby close to her chest.

"If anyone comes from the back, I'll tell you where to run." Eli gave the instruction as he reached for the doorknob on the front door. Did he just unlock it?

A ball of nerves lodged in her throat.

"If I go down, you run and grab a knife from the kitchen or the gun Phoenix left for you on the table. It's loaded."

Marion should probably look around to know where the weapons were, but she couldn't pull her gaze from Eli any more than she could steer her mind away from the visual he'd inspired. Of him being shot. Killed.

A pain, slow and burning, seared her chest.

"We've got a visitor."

She could barely hear Eli's voice. But she saw his hand reach out toward her and dribble the air like a basketball, signaling she should get down.

She lowered on her haunches and peered over the cushion that protruded above the back of the sofa.

Eli moved to the Christmas tree and crouched. He should be obscured from the door in that position.

Silence stretched through the room like an electric current waiting to explode. Even Herc had gone quiet.

Pounding broke the silence.

Marion jumped and ducked low behind the sofa, clutching the baby to her chest.

Hercules barked at the knocking.

Ding-dong.

The cheerful sound of the doorbell singsonged through the house with dramatic irony, eliciting more furious barking from Herc behind the study door.

Marion's heartbeat thundered in her ears just as loudly.

The baby moved her little hands, shifting her head against Marion's green sweater.

Please don't wake up. Don't wake up. A cry would tell the man a baby was there.

Marion lifted her head and craned her neck just enough to see over the sofa. Her eyes locked on the door.

The knob turned.

She stopped breathing.

The door slowly opened.

She crunched lower and pressed closer to the sofa. But she had to see. Had to be ready.

A man slowly stepped inside, a ski mask covering his face. His hand reached inside his jacket. For a gun?

"Hold it." Eli's forceful command made the man freeze.

"Take your hand out of your jacket, slowly. It'd better be empty."

But the man yanked his hand out, and a shot exploded from his gun.

Eli! Her heart's shriek somehow stayed inside as another shot erupted, throbbing her ears.

The man grabbed his arm and dropped his gun with an angry moan.

Eli got him?

Her gaze swung to the Christmas tree where Eli stood and walked out, looking quite healthy and handsome, the gun aimed at the intruder.

Relief soothed her panic as she watched him direct the man to raise his good arm.

Eli patted him down, apparently checking for other weapons.

Poor Herc barked more frantically than usual from the study. The loud shots had no doubt spooked him.

Marion's pulse started to slow as she stayed behind the sofa. Was it okay to come out now?

Two pops sounded, somewhere outside.

Gunshots?

Her heart seized.

Phoenix was out there. Alone.

TEN

"Eli." Marion propped up on her knees, making herself higher behind the sofa. "We have to help Phoenix."

Eli shook his head. "You're safer in the house. And she wanted me to stay here, remember?"

Marion tried to ignore the way the man in the frightening black ski mask stared at her. "But she could be hurt."

"She seems capable."

Eli's not very convincing vote of confidence did little to calm the concern pinching Marion's ribs. What if Phoenix had been shot? And the other man was headed for the house?

Eli directed the masked captive to kneel and put his hands behind his head. "What I wouldn't give for handcuffs right about now." Eli cast a glance in Marion's direction as if she might keep some on hand.

"This should suffice."

Eli's gun swung toward the voice that came from the hallway.

Phoenix's voice.

Relief surged through Marion, and she pushed to her feet

as the woman herself appeared at the start of the hallway that led to the back door.

Unruffled in her charcoal beanie, black jacket, and jeans, Phoenix's blond braid didn't even appear mussed. No signs of injury on her or Dag, who stood at her side, alert as he eyed the masked visitor. Phoenix held a piece of thin plastic in her fingers. Was that a zip tie?

"That'll do." A new note of respect seemed to undergird Eli's tone and expression as Phoenix walked over, and he took the zip tie with a nod.

"Good thing I wasn't one of the visitors." Phoenix watched Eli as he bound the man's hands.

Eli's mouth shifted into a smirk. "Pretty sure none of them can move that quietly."

"I eliminated one by the kennel. Other one fled."

Eli grimaced.

"He never came close enough to be taken out." Phoenix related the information with as bland a demeanor as if she were talking about what she had for dinner last night. "His snowmobile became stuck, and he dug it out while I was busy with his friend."

"What'd you do to him?" Eli asked the question as if he was afraid Phoenix had killed the man.

Would she have?

"He's unconscious for now. Looks like yours is worse off." Phoenix's remark prompted Marion to more closely assess the man kneeling in her living room. Blood seeped down his black jacket. It appeared to originate at his shoulder.

"I'll take a look at that." Marion carried the baby toward the kitchen, headed for the First Aid kit.

"Move him to the kennel first."

"The kennel?" Marion turned to Phoenix.

"We'll keep them in the training room."

Eli seemed to agree with Phoenix's plan, since he hefted the man up without argument.

"I'll take him." Phoenix glanced back at Marion. "Give Moore the baby and meet me at the kennel with your First Aid kit. Hurry."

Eli gave Marion a reassuring look as he took the baby.

Marion tabled her confusion and dashed to grab her kit and meet Phoenix at the kennel. She wanted to ask what Phoenix intended to do about the men she planned to leave in the training area. After all, they'd all survived the long-expected attack without getting hurt. Eli and the baby were safe. Phoenix was fine. Even Marion was safe.

Phoenix probably wanted to secure the men until the weather cleared enough for her or Eli to go to the police. Although Eli wouldn't want to do that because of the bad cop whose identity he didn't know.

She'd have to ask Phoenix about her plan for turning the men in to the authorities and getting the baby home. But she could hardly do that in front of the traffickers.

So she held her tongue while she cleaned and dressed the injured man's flesh wound and watched silently as Phoenix tied up both men with strong lead lines Marion used for the dogs. Phoenix locked the traffickers in the training room and then she, Dag, and Marion headed back to the house.

Wind whipped snow up into Marion's face as they stepped outside. The air was turning frigid. Powerful gusts lifted the snow and blew it to form a wall that blocked her view of the trees on the north side of her property.

The weather prediction had been right. High winds, drifting, and whiteouts in the afternoon.

Marion stuffed her ungloved hands in her jacket pockets and hurried to keep up with Phoenix's fast clip.

Marion readied to ask her burning questions as they entered the house.

Eli rose from the sofa to meet them, the baby awake and sitting with her back against his chest and his bulky arm supporting her tiny body underneath.

"It's time for me to take the child." Phoenix's declaration came before Marion could open her mouth.

"But why?" The question slipped out much differently than Marion had intended. "Isn't the danger over? You got them."

"Reinforcements will come."

"She's right." Eli looked at Marion. "There are more of them. And the one who got away will report back to the others."

"But..." Marion searched for some shred of positivity she could hang on to even as it rapidly slipped away. "That man didn't see you."

"No, but he heard the shots. Saw his buddies disappear. He'll figure I'm here and armed. Most normal folks around here wouldn't have met his boys with gunfire."

"They'll be better prepared the next time they come." Phoenix added the ominous statement like the final nail in the coffin of Marion's happy relief.

So this was it. The moment Eli would say he wasn't going to let Phoenix take the baby alone. And they would both leave her.

"How are you going to carry the baby out?" Eli's deep voice drew Marion's gaze, but he was looking at Phoenix.

He was going to let her take the baby? Alone?

Not a hint of surprise showed on Phoenix's face. She probably wasn't surprised. She'd predicted Eli would trust her. "Marion will help me rig a wrap with blankets."

He nodded. "We'd better get started."

Marion stared at him. "You're not going?"

He turned his head to look at her. "Of course not. I couldn't leave you alone here with those brutes coming."

Her pulse tripped. Did he care about her?

His eyebrows scrunched closer together. "Are you sure you won't leave? These are the kind of men who would hurt you just for kicks." His throat moved like he swallowed hard. "They could take you and…"

She shook her head even as fear pinched her oxygen supply. "Then they're also the kind who would harm or kill my dogs for fun. I can't leave them alone."

His gaze stayed on Marion's for slow seconds. Then he looked toward Phoenix.

"She's right." Phoenix's matter-of-fact tone was strangely calming. "I need to leave now. We'll park the snowmobiles in the kennel. Then I'll go as soon as the baby's ready." Phoenix looked at her watch. "Nearly one o'clock now. I'd expect the others to come after sunset. They won't want to do this in daylight."

Do what exactly? Marion's throat choked the question, preventing it from coming out.

Just as well. She was sure she didn't want to know the answer.

ELEVEN

A shiver passed over Marion's skin under her sweater sleeves as she turned away from the front window where Phoenix, the baby, and Dag in tow on a sled had just disappeared into a whiteout of snow. Her heart clenched at the thought of the baby out in that weather. But they'd wrapped her well, and Phoenix promised no harm would come to her.

Marion's gaze moved to the small gun on the coffee table. The one Phoenix had said Eli would show her how to use.

Her ribs pinched as she remembered what Phoenix had said right after that, her last words before she left.

"Protect yourself at all costs." She had stared into Marion's eyes with an intensity Marion had never seen on Phoenix's usually emotionless face. "These men will abuse you so horribly you'll wish you were dead. Do not let them take you alive."

Terror had gripped Marion from the inside at the same moment Phoenix suddenly grabbed her wrist. "If Moore turns, you'll have to fight him, too. Show no mercy. They won't."

Lily nudged Marion's hand with her dry nose. Sweet Lily.

Always there for whatever Marion needed. And right now, Lily knew Marion needed comfort. Calm.

Marion rubbed her sleeve, trying to rid her skin of the raised bumps as she tried to shed the doubt Phoenix's warning about Eli had planted in her mind. He wouldn't turn on her, would he?

She moved her hands to pet Lily instead, her fingers gliding over the familiar patchy skin of the closest friend she'd ever had. The dog pressed into Marion's leg, as if trying to transfer her peace and steadiness.

If only Lily could provide some clear thinking, too. But Marion couldn't believe Eli would ever hurt her. Not with the way he took care of the baby. And now he'd chosen to stay behind to protect Marion, even when the baby was gone. He was risking his life for her, Marion Ainsley, as if she were worth saving, worth caring about.

No one had ever done that before. No one had ever cared about her before.

"Well, the snowmobiles are hidden away." Eli's voice startled her as he came out from the back hallway.

She kept herself from jumping outwardly this time, though Herc let out a single bark, not bothering to rise from the sofa where he lay stretched across the cushions.

Lily trotted to Eli, and he rubbed her head before glancing back up.

"You okay?"

Marion nodded.

But he still watched her. She could feel the warmth of his attention without looking.

"I was just thinking about what Phoenix said before she left."

Eli chuckled, the deep, warm sound beckoning Marion to look at him. "I know what you mean."

Had Phoenix said something to him, too?

"She told me she expects you to be unharmed when she gets back. And the way she said it sounded awfully like a threat." A smile played on his lips. "She really cares about you."

Did she? Marion had always supposed Phoenix helped at Forever Home because she loved dogs. Or cared about creatures in need. And she'd said she was there to learn the training techniques, too.

But now that Marion thought about it, that wouldn't explain why Phoenix would've strategized to get Eli to stay with Marion. And why she'd have come up with a plan to keep Marion safe if the traffickers came.

"I can see why." Eli's voice, lower than before, drew Marion from her thoughts. "You're easy to care for."

Her heart lurched. How she'd longed to hear words like that her whole life. But Phoenix's warning about Eli lurked at the back of her mind. What if he was trying to play her, to manipulate the vulnerable little woman now that they were alone?

"Why did you stay?" The question emerged from Marion's dry throat as a near-whisper. "You could be risking your life."

His deep brown eyes roamed her face. "How could I not?"

She reached to check the wave of hair covering her scar.

Her fingers touched bare skin instead. Scarred, bumpy, ugly skin.

Horror roiled through her. She had tucked the hair behind her ear when she'd fashioned the wrap around Phoenix for carrying the baby.

Eli could see everything.

She spun away, her fingers trembling as she started to tug the strands of hair loose.

"Leave it." He gently rested his hand on her arm.

She turned her head slightly toward him. Why wouldn't he want it covered?

He met her gaze. He didn't shrink away. No disgust or even pity showed in his dark irises.

Her heart thumped as the direction of his focus returned to the scar.

"What happened?"

No one ever asked that. At least not without repulsion lacing the words.

She swallowed, working up the courage to answer. "I was told my mom's boyfriend did it."

Deep lines cut into Eli's forehead as his brows lowered.

"Maybe my father. He burned my face with a lighter because I cried too much."

Eli's eyes pressed shut in what looked like an instinctive wince, as if he was the one who had been hurt. When they opened again, pain reflected in the brown depths, pain that was echoed in the set of his mouth.

An ache cinched her ribs. Did he really feel something? For her sake?

"I don't remember it. I've just always looked like this." That pain, of always being as she was, she remembered well. It throbbed every day of her life.

Eli stepped close, shifting to match her angle so he faced her straight on.

Her breathing shallowed as he stood only inches away.

His hand reached up, toward her face.

He touched her cheek. The scarred cheek. The scar itself.

She closed her eyes as his fingers gently brushed over the scar tissue. No one had ever touched her there.

"I'm so sorry, Marion." His breath fanned her face, touching the scar as he spoke.

She opened her eyes.

His dark gaze poured into hers, awash with compassion,

protectiveness, and something she'd only seen in her favorite movies.

And that was the look she knew couldn't be real. Her imagination was running away with her again. Or he was pretending.

She pulled back and turned her head. "It's par for the course. No one's ever been able to love me. Especially with this." She swung her hand in the direction of the scar.

"No family?"

She shook her head. "Lots of foster homes, group homes. No family." She managed to look at him. Better to face the truth head on and put the brake on her silly fantasies before she got hurt. "I'm damaged goods. Not the kind of girl anyone can love."

A muscle twitched near his beard, and the vertical lines between his eyebrows deepened as he stared at her. "That's not true."

Hope flared in her chest. Was he going to say *he* loved her?

"God loves you."

Disappointment doused the hope like a splash of ice water. And he was wrong anyway. "Even God can't love me. That's obvious."

"Why do you think that?"

"Because He has plenty of better people to love. The most beautiful, the smartest, the strong, and..." She stopped herself from adding handsome men like Eli. She folded her arms over her torso. "He doesn't love me, and I don't blame Him. I have nothing to offer."

Eli opened his mouth, his features pinching like he was going to protest.

"No, it's true." She interrupted before he could say more nice things that only gave her false hope. "If He did love me,

I'd know it. I'd see it because He wouldn't have...let my life be like it is. Let me be like this."

Eli's eyes softened. "God doesn't love like people do, based on shallow, selfish things. And His best plan for us doesn't always look the way we figure it should."

Lily stepped in front of Marion, brushing along her knees.

Marion rested her hand on the furless side of Lily's face as the dog pressed into her.

"Why did you adopt Lily?"

The unexpected question jumped Marion's gaze to Eli. "I wanted to save someone no one else wanted." The one like her. Her ribs pinched as she remembered the deep throb of loneliness the night when she'd considered ending the pain, ending her life. But one of those horribly sad commercials had come on TV showing dogs in cages, needing to be rescued. "I went to a shelter and asked to see the dog who'd been there the longest."

Marion looked down at Lily as she stroked the face most people considered ugly.

Lily lifted her head and aimed her brown eyes up at Marion's face.

"Lily was on death row because of what mange had done to her face before she was picked up. No one wanted her." Tears pooled in Marion's eyes as she looked at the dog who had her heart. She was absolutely beautiful to Marion. The thought that she'd almost been—

"You chose her because she needed you."

Marion glanced up at Eli. "I guess I did."

"God does that, too, Marion. He loves you so much that He gave His life to choose you. He let Himself be killed for you, let His killers drive nails into His hands and feet. He hung from a cross for you." Eli took a small step toward her. "He did that so He could adopt you."

She straightened, watching Eli, but her mind searched the

words he'd said. How incredible it would be to accept them, to believe all of that was true. "Why would He do that for me?"

"Because that's the kind of God He is. He is love itself."

She stared at Eli. The blood running through her veins cooled, and her stomach hardened. Like the last time she was told a family who'd met her at the home was considering adoption. She'd been through it so many times before. The soaring hopes and the plunge into dark despair.

She slid her tongue over her dry lips. "It's hard to believe." She took in a fortifying breath. Good things weren't true for her. Not love or family. Adoption. She was grown now, so that was okay. She was okay. She had her canine family. She was happy. "We'd better get to the rest of the prep Phoenix told us to do, don't you think?"

"Sure."

Marion didn't have to look to hear the disappointment in Eli's voice.

Better that than another crushing blow to her heart.

TWELVE

"That should do it." Eli stepped out of the hallway that led to the back of the house, his gaze finding Marion. "Back door is secure."

She nodded. "I think the barricade in the study is ready, too."

"You added more?"

"Yes, I added the armchair, and my desk will fit in the remaining space by the door perfectly."

"Great. One thing left. Teaching you how to handle your gun."

Nerves tossed in her belly at the mention of the task she'd hoped Eli had forgotten. Her frantic gaze caught the clock on the wall. *6:00 p.m.*

"I need to feed the dogs." She glanced around for Lily and Herc, her unease growing at the sight of the altered living room—empty space where the sofa used to be, the coffee table set on its side, the windows boarded up like her house was condemned.

And only Lily looked at Marion from where she lay by the Christmas tree. Marion had forgotten Herc was out in the kennel where she'd put him earlier. Phoenix and Eli didn't want him barking in the study and drawing attention to Marion.

No matter, she needed to feed the kenneled dogs, too.

"Marion." Eli's tone carried a hint of amusement. "You've put this off long enough."

Heat surged to her cheeks. He'd noticed? She swallowed. She couldn't help it if she abhorred violence. There was a reason she stuck to watching romance movies.

"You can't go out in the dark anyway."

"I have to."

"Maybe I can do it. After I teach you how to handle the gun."

She met his gaze where a twinkle of humor undermined his otherwise determined expression. It was the humor that made her want to try. For him. "Okay." The word sounded like a strangled whisper, but he pounced on the opportunity.

"Great." He stalked to the kitchen counter, snatched up the gun, and was at her side seemingly before she could blink. Definitely before she was ready.

She tried to focus as he showed her technical aspects of the gun, including where the safety was and how to take it off. But his close proximity played havoc with her senses again, her pulse skipping at every glance he directed her way.

"I'm going to leave the safety on because we don't want to shoot anything right now. But I want you to practice holding the gun." He extended the handle—the grip —toward her.

Her heart rate sped up for a different reason as she stared at it.

"It's okay. You hopefully won't need to use it at all. But you need to know how to just in case."

Then his hand touched hers, lifting it so he could set the gun on her palm.

Her mouth dried to sandpaper under the onslaught of nerves and the rush of feelings this man was pumping through her system. But she somehow managed to close her hand around the gun.

"Now, I want you to aim at the clock on the wall as if you were going to shoot it." He stepped even closer.

Her heartbeat thudded in her ears as she raised the gun and pointed it at the clock.

"Good. You want two hands holding the weapon. Like this." The distance between them vanished, and he stood behind her, reaching his arms on either side of her, his hands gently cradling hers as he positioned them on the gun.

Then he stopped moving.

She stopped breathing.

But his breaths deepened beside her ear. He shifted his hands to her shoulders, and the suggestion was all she needed. Before she thought, she'd swiveled to face him, and his arms were around her, cradling, embracing as he searched her gaze.

"Do you believe in love at first sight?" His rough whisper tingled every nerve in her body.

It was like a line from the movies, the scenes she loved most. Could this really be happening? To her? She tried to find her voice. "I want to."

"Tell me you feel this, too." His eyes plunged into hers, the intensity in them frightening and thrilling at the same time. "I've wanted to hold you like this since that first night. I don't want to leave you. Ever."

Her pulse pounded in her ears, threatening to drown out the words she couldn't believe were for her.

"You're so courageous and kind and amazing..." His gaze traveled over her face. "And so beautiful."

She reached for her scar.

"All of you." The emphasis he put in the statement halted her movement. "Especially your heart. You're so pure and—"

Barks echoed from outside.

The kennel. It wasn't only Herc, who barked at anything.

Eli's head turned toward the front door. "Do they do that a lot?"

"Not—" The words stuck in her throat. She cleared it, her gaze dropping to the small gun she still held in her hand that lightly rested against his chest. "Not really. They could be hungry for dinner."

He lowered his arms and walked toward the front window —the only one in the living room they hadn't boarded up.

An ache seeped into her chest as the loneliness she was so used to wrapped around her in place of his embrace.

He pulled the curtain aside a microinch. "Lights out there. Flashlights." Eli's tone became grim as he looked at her.

Worry, foreboding, and anger skittered across his features in rapid succession before they settled into hard resolve.

Fear gripped her heart.

"They're here."

THIRTEEN

"It's time." Eli flicked the light switch on the other side of the door. The living room went dark. "Marion, you need to go." He hurried to hit the switch for the kitchen lights, dowsing them in darkness.

But she couldn't leave him. Not alone to fight the men. To risk his life for her. They could—

She heard his approach just before his big hands cupped her shoulders.

He gently guided her toward the study, and Lily casually fell into step beside Marion as if everything were normal.

"I can't." She stopped in the doorway, planting her feet as she swiveled to him. Her adjusting eyes took in the outline of his strong face. "I can't leave you a—"

"Please, Marion. Do what Phoenix planned. For me, okay?"

She froze as his hands slid down her arms and back up.

"And for Lily."

As if doing it for him wouldn't be enough to sway her.

"Okay." She leaned toward him with the whisper, longing to feel his arms around her one more time.

"Promise me you won't come out. No matter what."

She couldn't do that. Not as visions of the possible, horrific scenarios raced through her mind.

But he didn't wait for her response. He gently pushed her into the room and closed the door behind her and Lily.

"Lock it and get the barricade closed right away." His command easily traveled through the door, followed by the sound of his footsteps and a shuffling noise as he moved away. Probably getting into position crouched behind the coffee table, the boarded-up windows along the side of the house to his back.

Marion went around the desk she'd pulled close earlier, so she'd be able to slide it into the front gap of the long row of objects. Eli had dragged the heavier pieces into the study, lining up the sofa, bookcases, and dresser in a straight row from the far wall to the door. Phoenix had said no one could get through a barricade like this one. At least once the desk made the barricade complete.

Marion set Phoenix's gun on the desk and started to shove the heavy piece of furniture between the door and dresser.

But what if Eli needed her? She stopped pushing and straightened, catching her lip in her teeth. She'd never be able to rush out to help him if the desk was in the way.

Not like she knew how to do anything that would help in this situation. But she'd have to try, wouldn't she?

She pulled the desk back again, just enough for her to slip through to stand by the door.

She pressed her ear against the wood.

Nothing.

Holding her breath, she reached for the doorknob and gently turned, opening the door a crack. She leaned toward the opening and peered out.

The front door was still closed and locked.

She shifted to the side and opened the door a hair more.

Her eyes now fully adjusted to the darkness, she could make out the silhouette of Eli's head above the coffee table. And his gun, extended over the table as he watched the door.

The traffickers would have to enter there, since the back door and windows were barricaded and boarded up.

She looked toward the door again.

A shadow moved across the window.

Her breath caught.

The door flung open as if kicked.

A spark of light burst from a dark figure. A crack stung Marion's ears.

Her hand squeezed the doorknob, wanting to close it and hide, but she held her ground.

Flashes flared from Eli's gun as he returned fire.

The shots boomed, louder than the torrent of blood rushing in her ears.

Then they stopped.

She peered at the doorway.

Moonlight shone back at her through the rectangular opening no longer blocked by any dark figures.

Had they given up?

Maybe they were trying to get in at the back of the house. The thought pinched her ribs.

"Hey, Lamont." The gruff voice made Marion start. It came from somewhere beyond the front door. "We got five guys out here. Only one of you. How long you think you can hold out?"

Silence filled the house. Was *Lamont* Eli's undercover name?

"Longer than you can, I bet." Eli's tone oozed with bravado and cockiness. Traits she hadn't seen a hint of since he'd been with her.

A rough laugh that sounded like a scraper being dragged

across ice answered through the doorway. "I knew you had a death wish when you ran out with the kid, but man. Keep this up and I'm gonna enjoy ending you."

"Sounds like all you doin' is talking. I got bullets to do my talkin'."

"You outnumbered, boy. Give up, and maybe we'll kill you fast instead of the slow way."

"I see why you never went into advertising, Dirk. You couldn't sell crack to a crackhead."

"But I can kill you."

A mass of dark figures filled the doorway and shots exploded into Marion's home.

They'd rushed the door all at once.

Fiery panic pumped through her veins.

A body fell forward, but the shooting didn't stop. Another man slumped, tumbled into her living room.

The bullets kept raining on Eli from three remaining silhouettes in the doorway.

He suddenly pulled backward. No, a bullet threw him. He was shot.

Her heart jumped into her throat as fear seized her chest. She started to open the door farther, to go to him.

But she stopped herself. They would kill her. Or take her for a fate worse than death. And they'd kill Eli anyway. What could she do?

Terror cascaded through her as the shooting stopped, and she quietly shut the door.

She pushed the desk in place against the door, tears coursing down her cheeks.

Lily pushed into Marion's leg, and Marion slid down to the floor, her back against the hard side of the desk. Lily came close and nuzzled her face into Marion's chest, looking for the hug that always seemed to be much more for Marion than Lily.

Marion pressed her cheek to Lily's head and shivered.

"Protect yourself at all costs."

Phoenix's warning rang in Marion's ears, but her heart's cry drowned them out. She only wanted to be with Eli.

But all she could do was hide, helpless as three dark figures invaded her home.

FOURTEEN

"Where's the baby?"

Marion stiffened at the sharp tone from the man Eli had called Dirk. He'd been interrogating Eli for several minutes.

"I told you it ain't here." Every time that Eli responded was a comfort. It meant he was alive and able to talk. But the growing anger in Dirk's voice churned Marion's stomach. Anger like that led to violence.

"Go find it." Dirk's command was apparently directed at one or both of the men with him.

A noise, like something shaking, came from above Marion's head. She shifted to her knees, away from the desk, and looked at the door.

The knob jiggled.

She froze. Didn't breathe.

"Why's the door locked?" Dirk spewed out the question as if he might shoot whoever answered.

"Not sure it is." Eli's voice was as calm as a frozen lake. "Might be jammed. It was like that when I got here."

A snort came from someone, probably Dirk. "You stashed the baby in there."

"Right. That's why you hear all that crying."

"You probably drugged it."

Now it was Eli's turn to grunt. "Like I know the safe dose to give a baby. You think I'd risk killing it? It's worth way too much alive, man."

"Then where is it?" Dirk yelled the question, sending a tremble through Marion.

"Why should I tell you?" Eli didn't sound frightened in the slightest. "You'd muscle in on my profits."

"Or I could just shoot you again. Someplace that'll hurt a lot worse than your shoulder."

Marion's chest squeezed, pinching the air from her lungs. Eli should tell them the cover story he'd come up with, shouldn't he? She knew he couldn't spill everything at once or they wouldn't believe him, but he could get hurt by making them drag it out of him.

"The boss said to bring you back. Dead or alive." Footsteps clomped. Was he moving closer to Eli? To shoot something vital? Something painful?

"All right."

Marion sagged with relief as Eli gave in.

"I left the baby with this chick I know before I left the city, after the boys went off the road."

"That chick you took home from Brady's Friday night?"

"Yeah."

Marion's stomach clenched. That wasn't the kind of cover story she'd thought Eli had in mind when he'd mentioned he had one.

Dirk made a dirty comment about Eli's fling, and Eli laughed. Hurt joined the tension in Marion's belly, creating a nauseating combo.

But Eli was only playing a role. He was trying to control the situation and not blow his cover.

She drew in a breath through her nose as she tried to

convince herself he didn't really have a mistress stashed somewhere.

"I'll take you to the baby if we split the profits. Fifty-fifty." Eli's voice took on a quality she didn't recognize. A dark edge, a sinister amusement that usually accompanied the cruelty she'd seen from the worst people in her life. "I got a buyer already lined up." The eagerness in his tone pushed bile up her throat. "He wants more if I can get 'em, so I hope you got more where this one came from."

Footsteps sounded on the carpet. One of the others coming back?

"There was only the one." A different voice, masculine but pitched higher, responded. "I just saw it in a car and grabbed it."

"In a car? Where?"

"Celebration Foods."

The grocery store? Dismay twisted in Marion's torso. The poor mother. Though far worse for the baby.

"We could do that again. Look for more babies left in cars." Was Eli actually giving them ideas for how to kidnap more children?

"Hey, Dirk." A third voice called out as steps moved near the door. "There's a chick living here. Found clothes and makeup upstairs."

Oh, no. Phoenix had said they'd figure out she was there sooner or later. There was nothing they could do about that. But the barricade should hold.

"No one was here when I came. Sure wish there had been a chick here."

A couple of the men snickered at Eli's joke.

"Nice try, Jackson." Dirk didn't sound amused. "Tell him what you saw when you were here before, Ahmod."

"Somebody out by the other building with those dogs

barking inside." The guy with the higher, younger-sounding voice answered. "Too small to be Lamont."

"Like a girl, maybe." Dirk finished the thought for the guy. "Where is she, Jackson?"

"Not here, obviously." Eli was still trying to bluff them. Maybe that meant he really was the good guy she thought he was. He was trying everything he could to keep her hidden.

"Maybe she out in that other building." The third guy's suggestion made Marion's skin crawl.

The dogs. She gripped the edges of the desk, ready to pull it out of position.

She'd give herself up before they went out there. Before they could hurt any one of the dogs. She'd told Phoenix as much, and she hadn't seemed surprised at all.

"Check it out." Dirk's order dropped her stomach to her toes.

She started to tug the desk.

"What was that?" The younger guy was closer to the door than she thought.

She stopped. Her pulse pounded in her ears.

"I heard something in there."

"What do you say, Lamont?" Dirk's tone took on a sick amused quality that sent shivers snaking up her arms. "Should we use that door for target practice?"

Marion tried to swallow but nearly coughed when the saliva caught in her dry throat. She pressed her hand over her mouth.

"If they open fire, hit the floor by the furniture and have Lily lie down."

Phoenix's instruction rang in Marion's memory.

Lily pressed her shoulder into Marion's leg. What if a bullet hit Lily?

Marion should go out there. Give—

"No." Eli's voice stopped her short. "She's in there."

Marion let out a breath. Eli knew how important the dogs were to her. Or maybe he was afraid a bullet would find her despite Phoenix saying it was unlikely if she did as instructed. Either way, she was grateful.

Dirk chuckled—a sinister, awful sound that reminded Marion of the men who used to visit her mother and supply her drugs. "Let me guess. You wanted to keep her for yourself?"

"Not hardly. She barricaded herself in there when I was sleeping this morning." Disgust filled Eli's tone. "As if I'd want to touch her."

What was he saying? Marion put her hand on Lily's head as she tried to hold on to what she thought was true. Eli was only telling them he didn't want to abuse or traffic her. That was a good thing. Though it wouldn't fit his cover. Wouldn't he want to pretend he was going to take her and sell her?

"Trying for sainthood all the sudden?" Dirk's sardonic question prompted laughs from the other men. "I bet you already got her posted online. How many customers you got?"

"No way. Nobody could make money off her. She got the ugliest scar I ever seen over half her face."

All warmth drained from Marion as she stood rooted in place. That couldn't be Eli's voice. Not saying those words. The ones she'd heard so many times.

"Some customers don't care."

"Oh, they'd care about this one. It's gross, man. Makes her look like a freak." Each word stabbed into her heart like a knife wielded in Eli's hand.

There was nothing inauthentic about the way he said them. Sincerity and truth rang in every syllable. He wasn't faking. Not now.

How could she have believed he could love her? Of course

he thought she was ugly. No man could ever think of her romantically. She knew that.

He was only being kind when he'd touched her scar, when he'd said all those lovely things before—

Or maybe he'd been playing a role? Isn't that what under-cover cops did every day? Maybe it served him or his plan to befriend her, to charm her into caring for him. Or maybe he couldn't stop pretending because he'd been doing it so long.

The bile she'd tamped down bubbled back up, the bitter taste hitting the back of her mouth. She stumbled to the corner farthest from the door and sank to the carpet in front of the built-in bookcase.

Lily lay beside her, the warmth of her body against Marion's leg devoid of the comfort she usually provided.

Muffled voices sounded in the distance, but Marion could barely hear them, could scarcely breathe or think past the pain. She knew better than to dream, even for a moment, that someone could love her.

The pulsing, searing throb started in her heart and spread outward, winding through her chest and seeping into all her being like a deadly disease that would kill her.

What a relief that would be.

FIFTEEN

The moaning of the stormy wind outside was like the echo of Marion's heart as it sank in on itself, wishing, waiting for death. This had been her fate, her life for so long. Loneliness, rejection, pain. She couldn't do it anymore.

Maybe the traffickers would shoot through the walls into the room and end her miserable life.

Lily abruptly stood and nuzzled Marion's face, her tail wagging.

"Lily, don't." Marion gently pushed Lily's nose away. Even the dog who always knew what to do for Marion couldn't fix this.

Something clattered to the floor.

"Lily." Marion hissed the name in a hushed tone, though she should probably go ahead and yell, attract the bullets that would be her way out.

She leaned forward to see what Lily's tail must have knocked off a shelf. Marion had placed Christmas decorations in every nook and cranny throughout the whole house. All the good it did her. This might be the most horrible Christmas she'd ever had.

A small object lay on the gray carpet about a foot from the shelves.

Marion reached for it and settled back into the corner.

She opened her hand and stared at the ceramic figurine of baby Jesus in a manger—the only Christmas gift she'd ever received.

She could still see the woman's smile. What was her name?

Mrs. Isaksson.

Marion had only seen her once when she was ten years old. But she'd never forgotten. She couldn't forget the only person who hadn't reacted to her scar.

Mrs. Isaksson had singled Marion out from all the other kids to spend time with while her church group visited the home and handed out gifts.

The woman with blond hair, blue eyes, and a kind smile had given Marion a wrapped gift. For her.

Marion hadn't opened it at first because she was waiting for the dismay to show on the woman's face now that she'd gotten close enough to see the scar.

But Mrs. Isaksson kept smiling and touched Marion's shoulder as she said it was okay to open the gift right then if she wanted to.

Marion tore into the package as fast as she could, afraid it would be yanked from her grasp before she could see what was inside.

But no one stopped her from opening it and holding the beautiful, painted figurine of a baby.

"Do you know who that baby is?" Mrs. Isaksson still smiled, but Marion's pulse double-timed as she tried to find the right answer so the lady wouldn't take the present back. But she didn't know the right answer, so she stayed silent.

And Mrs. Isaksson told her who the baby was supposed to be. Someone named Jesus who was really God.

The woman sat in her fancy clothes beside Marion on the ratty sofa as she told the story. "He came as a baby and grew into a man who died for His children, to save them from punishment for the bad things they'd done."

"Who are His children?" The question slipped out before Marion thought. Her breath caught as she waited to see if the woman would become angry.

But she didn't. Her smile grew more beaming and beautiful as she answered. "His children are the ones He chose to be His."

"You mean He adopted them? Like a forever family?" Warmth Marion didn't understand filled her insides.

"Yes. He came back to life, and He's alive right now, getting ready to bring His children home." Mrs. Isaksson covered Marion's hand with her own on the inches of cushion between them. "Do you know how to tell if He's chosen to adopt you as His daughter?"

Someone might want to adopt her? The warmth exploded in a burst of heat that made Marion bounce in her seat. "How?"

"If you believe He loves you and ask Him to save you and forgive all the bad things you've done, then you'll know. Because you can only do that if He chose to adopt you first."

Marion tilted the figurine in her hand as the memory of Mrs. Isaksson's words faded away. She'd wanted to believe what the woman had said back then. But she couldn't. Not after Mrs. Isaksson had left, and Marion still wasn't adopted. Not then. Not ever.

She stared at the baby in the manger. Her finger traced the detailed curves and painted features of the tiny infant. Just like the little girl Eli had rescued. The figurine was so lifelike, right down to the tiny hands that lifted in the air.

The hands they'd put nails into.

Eli's words rushed to her mind. *"He let Himself be killed for you, let His killers drive nails into His hands and feet."*

Marion winced. Images appeared in her head before she could stop them. The violence of nails driven into flesh. Of deep wounds that would never heal even if He survived.

He'd have scars.

The realization jolted through her like an electrical shock.

"He did that so He could adopt you." Eli's voice echoed in Marion's memory as her heart pounded.

He'd taken scars for her.

Tears stung her eyes as the burst of hope that had died long ago exploded within.

She'd told Eli she would know if God loved her. But she'd ignored the proof. The scars Jesus must have in His hands and feet. The evidence that He could love her even with her scars, her ugliness.

He voluntarily took such scars for her.

He loved her.

The tears tracked down her cheeks as she leaned her head back against a shelf.

He chose her. Like she chose Lily, Jesus picked her not because she was beautiful or attractive, but because she needed Him. And because He could love her despite her scars.

The almost unbelievable, glorious truth seeped into her soul, washing away the despair that had tried to destroy her.

This wasn't a dream or a hope that would be dashed. It was forever. She knew beyond a shadow of doubt that He'd chosen her. That He'd adopted her. Because He had just done the impossible.

He'd helped her see clearly what she couldn't before. He enabled her to believe He loved her.

So this was what adoption felt like. What love felt like.

A smile stretched Marion's mouth, letting her taste the

saltiness of the tears that rolled over her lip. But they were good tears now, happy tears, overflowing from the real love that flooded her soul.

It was everything she'd ever dreamed of.

A loud whack cut through Marion's joy and jerked her gaze to the door.

"Hey, man." Why did Eli's voice sound so breathless? "That ain't no way to treat a guy when he's trying to cut you in on a deal. Keep that up, and I won't give you any of the action. I'll keep the baby and the chick for myself."

"You gonna be dead, Lamont. And I'm gonna take them both." Dirk growled with anger more intense than before. "After we have some more fun, right boys?"

Another thud. And a grunt. From Eli?

Were they beating him?

Marion scrambled to her feet and moved toward the door.

SIXTEEN

Marion's pulse sprinted as she reached the desk that blocked the door. She couldn't just hide and let them hurt him. Kill him.

"I think you knocked him out." The younger man spoke the words that seized Marion's breath.

"Too bad." Dirk snarled. "It was just getting fun. We'll have to finish him off here then."

Marion's heart lurched. Her gaze locked on the gun she'd left on the desk. Could she use it? For Eli?

Her chest swelled with the answer. She had to believe he cared for her, too. He might not love her in the way she'd imagined, but she knew he cared. He'd stayed behind for her, and now he could die for her. She couldn't let that happen.

"You know where the chick with the baby lives?"

"I guess so." The third guy answered Dirk's question in a bored tone.

"Then we don't need him."

Marion gripped the edges of the desk and pulled, thankful for the carpet that muffled the sound.

"You gonna shoot him or take him back alive?"

"He's too ambitious." Dirk's voice moved slightly farther away. Closer to Eli? "The boss will thank me."

He was going to shoot Eli.

Something powerful surged through Marion's torso and into her muscles as she scooted around the desk and snatched the gun.

She switched off the safety, then gave Lily a hand signal to wait as she opened the door a crack.

The three men stood grouped in her living room, their backs to her as they looked at a body on the floor beyond the two who had fallen in from the door earlier.

Eli. He lay sprawled on his back at their feet, closest to the bearded older guy she assumed was Dirk.

The same man who held a gun. And aimed it at Eli.

"No!" The scream ripped from Marion's throat as she flung open the door and pointed her gun at Dirk's leg.

She pulled the trigger.

The gun jerked in her hands, jumping higher than she'd aimed as the boom pierced her ears.

But Dirk let out a roaring yell.

She'd hit him.

The moment seemed to freeze in time.

Then chaos broke loose.

Eli leaped up and rammed into Dirk, taking him down at the knees.

Another man pointed his gun at Eli.

A bark startled Marion as Lily darted through the doorway and dashed for the man with the gun. She jumped and snagged his jacket in her teeth with a growl.

He spun around, trying to reach Lily behind his back.

Marion directed her weapon at him. She had to protect Lily. But she couldn't shoot without—

The front door burst open, and a tan blur catapulted from the darkness as shots rang out.

Dagian?

The dog snarled as he launched at the younger man Marion just realized was aiming a gun at her. He bit down on the guy's leg, making him shriek.

Someone tumbled into the room, rolled, leaped to her feet. Phoenix.

She slipped around the man Lily was keeping occupied and twisted his arm in a hold that made him drop to his knees.

Lily let go and trotted back to Marion as a small woman she hadn't seen arrive pointed a gun at the younger guy Dag had subdued.

The two armed women made quick work of moving the men toward the wall and having them all kneel. Dirk seemed to find the task challenging with the thigh wound that bled through his jeans.

Marion watched, her mind struggling to grasp what had just happened. The fact she'd put the wound in the man's leg. The fact it might be over.

"Are you okay?" Eli. His breath brushed her ear, his fingers touching hers as he gently took the gun from her grasp.

She turned toward him, must have leaned in, because she was suddenly wrapped in his arms. Safe.

She buried her face in his strong chest as tears escaped her eyes.

He cradled her close, his hand gently rubbing her back.

She sniffed, trying to rein in the emotion.

He pulled back slightly, dipping his head toward hers. "Hey, it's okay. It's over."

She nodded, but his comforting words seemed to prompt more tears.

"Marion, what is it?" His thumb went to her cheek, wiping the tears with such tenderness they just came faster.

"You know I didn't mean anything I said to them about you, right? I was only trying to—"

"Save me." She smiled as she lifted her hand off his chest to brush away her tears. "I know."

"Everyone all right?" Phoenix's steady tone had never sounded sweeter, even if she was interrupting a moment with Eli that Marion wouldn't mind continuing.

Marion's cheeks warmed as she realized the position they were in—Eli holding her against his chest in view of Phoenix and everyone. He was so kind to comfort her. But she didn't want others getting the wrong idea about his kindness like she had.

She took a step back and angled toward Phoenix, hoping her embarrassment didn't show. "I'm fine." She glanced at Eli, who watched her with an expression she couldn't quite read. "Oh, but Eli was shot."

More heat rushed to her face. How could she have forgotten and spent all that time crying all over him when he'd been shot? Some nurse she would've been. He'd been punched, too. A small cut marked his cheekbone, and that probably wasn't the extent of his injuries.

Phoenix jerked a nod. "I see that. Agent Nguyen called for an ambulance. Might take them awhile, but the roads are becoming more passable."

"Where's the baby?" Eli faced Phoenix.

"Safe. With a social worker Agent Nguyen trusts."

The petite woman with black hair and a fierce demeanor marched toward them, her prisoners bound and lined up along the wall behind her.

"FBI?" Eli looked at the woman as she stopped in front of them.

She nodded and extended her hand for what looked like a very firm shake with Eli. "Special Agent Nguyen. I've got more agents on their way. ETA twenty minutes."

"I understand you placed the baby with a social worker?"

"Yes. She's trustworthy."

"I found out the baby was stolen from a parked car at Celebration Foods."

"Good. That'll help us get the child home quickly, maybe tonight." She pulled a cell phone from her jacket pocket. "Some Christmas present, huh?" She spun away and pressed the phone to her ear as she stalked toward the kitchen.

Phoenix returned to the prisoners, scanning them as if checking for any signs they were trying to escape.

"I forgot."

Marion looked at Eli to see him checking his watch.

"It's almost Christmas. Just a matter of hours now."

Lily trotted toward Marion from the kitchen where she must've been trying to get Agent Nguyen's attention.

Marion squatted down and welcomed the dog in her arms, rubbing her sweet girl's patchy coat. "Good girl, Lily." The dog didn't seem disturbed or nervous about all that had happened. "I can't believe you bit that man's jacket."

"Her timing couldn't have been better." Eli's comment drew Marion's gaze.

"But she's never bitten anyone or even anyone's clothing in her life. At least not since I've known her." Marion shook her head as she stroked Lily's face. "She's the gentlest dog in the world."

"Well, I'm glad she and you decided to use some weapons when you did."

Marion stood as Eli gave her and Lily a smile. "You two saved my life."

Marion shook her head. "You saved ours."

He rubbed the back of his neck with his hand and cast her a glance that looked almost shy. "You know, wrap-up here will take some time. The FBI agents will want to debrief us, and I suppose the medics will want to check us out."

"They'd better examine you. You need attention."

A smile curved his full lips, and he took a step closer. "The only attention I need is yours."

Her pulse skittered. Had he really just said that?

His hands went to her upper arms, gently sliding over her sweater. "I hope I'm here past midnight. Because there's no one I'd rather spend Christmas with than you."

Her heart pounded hard against her ribs as she stared into his eyes and saw sincerity there.

But she didn't want to imagine anything that wasn't true. Imagine love where there wasn't any.

It was okay if he didn't love her. She didn't need it so much now.

Her heart didn't feel like it might break if he didn't love her, if he didn't mean what she hoped he did. No, it felt solid and whole. Full of God's love.

Joy shaped her lips with a smile. "Christmas will be different for me this year."

Those dark eyebrows lifted as he watched her.

"I've been adopted."

His brow furrowed.

She let out a light laugh at his adorably puzzled expression. "God adopted me. I believe in Jesus. That He loves me and everything you told me. I know it's true now."

His mouth stretched in a smile so big she thought it might burst through his beard. "Oh, Marion." He engulfed her in a hug so warm and sweet she didn't want it to end. He stopped too soon and stepped back, his big grin still in place. "That's the best news I've ever heard. The Bible says that 'in love' God 'predestined us for adoption to Himself.' You're a child of God now."

Did the Bible really say that? A thrill tracked through her veins.

Eli's smiled faltered, and he pressed his lips together. "I

hope..." He took in a visible breath. "I hope to be part of your family, too."

Her heart stopped.

"I want to spend Christmas with you, I want to love you—"

"Moore." Agent Nguyen's sharp tone cut him short, leaving Marion feeling as though she were suspended in the air mid-fall. "I need to interview you to get all the details."

Eli gently squeezed Marion's arm. "I'll be back." He pulled his gaze away, slowly, as if he didn't want to, then followed the agent to the kitchen.

Marion watched him go as her pulse restarted, skipping wildly. Had he really meant he wanted to be with her?

Could he...love her?

Something warm bumped into her leg. Marion glanced down to see Lily tilt her head to look into Marion's face. Just the reminder Marion needed—of the most wonderful truth of all.

She was already loved beyond her wildest dreams.

EPILOGUE

Marion stepped outside onto the porch with a basket of Christmas gifts for the dogs slung over her arm.

Lily dunked her face in the drift to the left of the front door while Herc started gulping the white stuff like it was ice cream.

Large, fluffy snowflakes fell gently from the sky. Bright sunlight beamed down on the flakes that covered the ground, kicking up diamond sparkles as far as Marion could see. Peace and silence blanketed the stunning white landscape.

A perfect Christmas morning, and not only because of the beautiful weather.

As soon as she had gotten out of bed that morning, she'd dug out the dusty Bible she'd found in her old house when she had moved in. Wanting to see how Eli and Mrs. Isaksson knew about God adopting people, she looked up *adoption* in the concordance and found the verse Eli had quoted yesterday. That passage also said God chose her before she was born, even before the foundations of the world. The awesomeness of it gave her goosebumps.

She'd found other amazing verses, too. Including some about God never leaving her and always being with her.

She'd had her last Christmas alone.

The incredible thought buoyed her steps as she clomped through drifts with the dogs and arrived at the kennel.

"Merry Christmas, kids!" She hurried to each kennel and wished every dog a *merry Christmas* as she gave them their special gifts. She took the time to unwrap each flavored chew toy by the recipient so he or she could enjoy the moment to the fullest.

Lily and Herc had already received their Christmas presents at the house, but she'd never know it from the way Herc drooled as he watched the other dogs enjoy their gifts.

He suddenly swung away and barked.

Someone moved just inside the back door.

A woman in a charcoal beanie and dark clothes, her dog by her side.

Phoenix.

Marion released the breath she'd been holding and stepped out of Oliver's kennel, latching it behind her. "Merry Christmas, Phoenix." She smiled as her friend neared.

Phoenix gave her a nod.

What was Phoenix's story? She didn't seem thrilled by Christmas either. The way Marion used to be. Maybe Marion should tell her about God's love and what Jesus did for her.

"The traffickers flipped." Phoenix spoke before Marion could decide what to say. "They gave the FBI evidence on the higher-ups, including their contact at the police department. The FBI brought them all in, and agents are recovering victims now."

"That's wonderful." Marion silently thanked God that she wasn't the only one being saved this Christmas. "What about the baby?"

"Reunited with her family this morning. Her name is Joy."

Tears blurred Marion's eyes. Joy. The baby had a name. And a bright future. Joy was exactly the emotion that welled up inside Marion for the sweet girl and her family. "Thank you for helping her, Phoenix."

"I plan to help more people. You can be part of that."

Marion blinked at the unexpected transition.

"We can make a difference. Save more dogs and humans."

"That sounds wonderful. But how?"

"We team up. You find dogs to rescue that have the right aptitude, and we'll train them for K-9 work using your positive methods. They'll be trained with skills we can use to save human lives."

Marion stared at Phoenix as the idea struck a chord in her own heart. She'd always wanted to help people and dogs. She thought she had to stick with only dogs, since people didn't want her around. But this way... "I'm in."

"We'll start with Dag." Phoenix continued as if she'd expected that answer.

Marion looked at the dog who stood at Phoenix's side, watching Marion with his piercing blue eyes.

"He has natural protective instincts, but he needs to hone them."

"I agree. He's very smart and trainable, and there was no missing his desire to protect last night."

"I'd like to beef up his tracking skills, too." Phoenix met Marion's gaze with a hint of emotion, maybe determination, in her usually unreadable eyes. "I'm going to start an agency of women handlers and the K-9s we train. We'll offer protection, detection, and rescue operations."

Wow. Marion had no idea all that had been going on in Phoenix's mind. Were these big plans the reason why she'd sought Marion out in the first place? She'd never breathed a word of it in all these months.

"Sounds amazing." Almost as amazing as Marion was starting to realize Phoenix was. A gun-toting woman who could take down armed men with her bare hands and trek through a blizzard to save a baby. Who was Phoenix?

The question echoed the one Eli had asked her and returned her thoughts to the man who hadn't been far from them all morning.

She yearned to ask Phoenix where he was, if she'd seen or heard how he was doing. If he was recovering from being shot and beaten. After Agent Nguyen had taken him away for the interview, Marion hadn't seen him again. One of the other agents told her he'd gone to the FBI office in Minneapolis. She'd hoped he might return after he was done, but fatigue had eventually demanded she go to bed once all the agents had cleared out.

She bit back the urge to see if Phoenix knew anything about how Eli was as she finished presenting the final gift to Pip, a tiny chihuahua she gave a miniature bone.

"Have you seen Moore?"

Marion paused in closing the door to Pip's run behind her. She hadn't thought Phoenix would bring up Eli. Did she know Marion was thinking about him? "No. I don't think he'd come here, though." Her pulse skipped a beat. Did Phoenix have reason to think otherwise?

"Last I saw him was late last night. He was at the FBI office when I left."

"Oh. Was he okay?" Marion stepped away from the kennel and clipped leashes to Herc's and Lily's harnesses, trying to act casual while her stomach clenched.

"The paramedics patched him up and directed him to go to the hospital to get checked out. Nothing that won't heal, I'm told."

"That's good." Very good, according to the relief that flowed through her.

Marion didn't dare say anything else, anything that would risk showing Phoenix how much she cared about the man she'd probably never see again.

Phoenix would likely think she was silly and foolish.

Marion and Phoenix finished feeding and caring for the dogs together in silence, then locked up the kennel and headed for the house.

A low growl came from Dag, and Herc echoed him with a loud woof.

Marion stopped in the deep snow and looked ahead.

"You have a visitor." Phoenix continued walking, apparently not alarmed by the darkly clothed figure outside the front door of the house.

Then he turned in their direction.

Eli.

Marion's heart leaped, bouncing against her ribs. Clearly, she still cared about him more than she thought.

But he wouldn't feel that way for her. And that would be okay. She would be okay.

She ran the bolstering reminders through her head as Herc pulled her through the drifts, eager to greet Eli.

Lily stayed at Marion's side but kept throwing glances up at Marion, showing she'd like to move much faster toward the visitor.

The dogs wagged their whole bodies as they reached the porch where Eli waited, wearing his black beanie with a navy blue winter jacket and jeans.

A grin split his beard as he squatted down to greet the dogs. "Hey, guys! You miss me?"

They licked his face, earning a laugh that kicked up flutters in Marion's stomach.

He looked up at her, and his eyes seemed to soften.

"Merry Christmas."

"Y—" Her suddenly dry throat wouldn't let out the response. She cleared it. "You, too."

His last words to her the night before clanged in her memory. *I want to love you.*

But as she'd reminded herself that morning, more than once, wanting to love was not the same thing as actually loving her. He'd probably been about to explain why he couldn't.

Crunching in the snow behind Marion jerked her back to the moment she was in now. She swiveled to look.

Phoenix was a few feet away, leaving with Dag.

"Phoenix, wait. Do you want to come inside for hot chocolate or breakfast?" It was the least she could do for the woman who'd visited her on Christmas morning, helped with the dogs, and saved her life the day before.

"There's somewhere I have to be."

"Okay." Marion would have to find another way to make it up to her, if she ever could. "I hope you have a wonderful Christmas. And thank you for everything."

Phoenix gave one of her short nods and walked away, Dag jumping through the drift Phoenix broke through with ease.

"Does that invitation count for me, too?" Eli's deep, roughened voice tickled her insides at the same time it seemed to draw her to him.

She tried for a normal, non-lovesick smile as she faced him. "Of course. Come in." She brushed past him to open the door, and the dogs jogged inside, immediately picking up their new bones and settling down to chew on them.

"All the gifts are gone."

Marion turned around to see Eli's gaze aimed at the bare skirt under the Christmas tree. "They were for the dogs."

A twinkle lit Eli's mahogany eyes as he smiled at her. "You care about everyone, don't you?"

Sometimes too much. Her throat clogged with the dashed hopes she shouldn't feel. What had she expected? That he'd take her in his arms and kiss her the moment he saw her?

She forced a casual shrug. "Would you like breakfast or hot chocolate?"

"How about both?"

"Sure thing." Disappointment crept into her voice, though she tried to keep it at bay. She swung away and headed toward the kitchen. At least she'd have the company of a friend on Christmas morning. And friendship should be enough. That was more than she'd ever had.

A hand on her arm stopped her just before she'd reached the counter. "Marion." Eli's voice sounded thicker than before.

She slowly rotated toward him, and he released his hold.

But his gaze gripped her instead with an intensity that sent a shiver through her. "I need to tell you what I was trying to say last night."

Oh, no. The explanation about why he couldn't love her.

He took a step toward her. "I know this seems fast, and I don't want to scare you."

Her breath caught. What exactly was he going to say?

"But I've never felt this way about anyone before." He took another step and closed the distance between them, his large hands going to her upper arms. "We're meant for each other, Marion."

Her heart surged, trying to beat its way out of its cage, even as her mind struggled to believe he'd actually spoken those words.

"I want to spend Christmas with you and every day with you for the rest of my life."

Was he saying what she—

"I want to marry you. If you'll have me." His hands tightened on her arms as his eyes filled with hope and—she dared to believe—love. "I'll do whatever it takes to get you to choose me. Because I love you, Marion."

Wow. Her heart swelled as a smile stretched her mouth from ear to ear. This was so much more incredible than she'd ever dreamed even from the best romantic scenes in her favorite movies.

Joyous tears pooled in her eyes, but she blinked them back. "I love you, too, Elijah Moore. And yes. I choose you."

He smiled and cradled both sides of her face in his hands as he lowered his head toward hers.

As she closed her eyes to receive her very first kiss, she finally knew why so many Christmas movies were about love.

Thanks to God adopting her and choosing Eli and Marion for each other, this Christmas was the start of her new life. And every day of it would be filled with love.

Turn the Page for a Special Sneak Peek of

GUARDIANS UNLEASHED, BOOK 1

HIDDEN DANGER

AVAILABLE NOW

HIDDEN DANGER
CHAPTER ONE

Cora Isaksson's pulse jerked with her arm when Jana tugged hard to the right. The golden retriever never pulled on her leash unless she caught scent of one of two things—narcotics or a human in need of rescue.

Jana tugged toward a black suitcase parked upright next to a man in the baggage claim of Minneapolis International Airport.

"Get that dog away from my luggage." The middle-aged, heavyset man had a smudge of dark hairs on his head and a long, sagging mustache that shaped his mouth into a severe frown.

Cora's mind raced. She and Jana were off the clock, finished logging in their hours searching for narcotics at Departures. The usual TSA officer who accompanied her had left, and Cora had handed in her radio for the day.

But Jana sat next to the man's suitcase and aimed her big brown eyes up at Cora.

She'd found drugs.

Cora swallowed. She glanced past the scattered crowds of people, her gaze finding the nearest glass exit doors.

A security guard, Frank O'Donnell, stood by the exit, talking to a woman with suitcases piled in a precarious stack.

Cora should be able to get help from Frank if the traveler didn't cooperate.

"I said, get it away from me." The man's voice lowered as he grabbed the long handle of his suitcase and started walking. Toward the exit.

"Sir, wait." Cora grabbed a handful of treats from her pocket on autopilot and gave them to Jana as she hurried after the escaping passenger.

A younger man stepped into the mustached man's path, halting him abruptly.

They appeared to exchange some words, then glared at Cora as she approached with Jana.

The golden smelled the suitcase, her feathered tail swishing with excitement.

"Sir, I'm afraid you're going to have to stay and allow your suitcase to be searched." Cora's voice trembled slightly as trepidation coursed through her veins. Confronting a suspect without backup from an officer was risky, but she couldn't let him go. "This is a narcotics detection K-9, and she has identified there may be illegal narcotics in your suitcase."

"I don't care what you or your dog think. You can't stop me from leaving." The man nodded to his companion, and they turned to leave again.

"No." Cora's heart thudded against her ribs, as if an instinctive warning of self-preservation. But she darted in front of the two men, using Jana's wagging body to help block them. "I'm sorry, but you can't leave." She started to turn toward Frank.

Someone grabbed her arm and yanked her backward.

Cora gasped.

"Don't you dare." The younger man leveled the threat in a low growl. He stood just behind her to one side, his body an uncomfortable inch or two away from hers. He squeezed her arm as he leaned in, an odor that suggested he hadn't bathed in a while assaulting her nostrils.

"Feel this?" He pressed something hard into her back through her jacket.

She held her breath. She'd never had a gun poking her before, but somehow, she knew without a doubt what it was. *Father, please help me.*

"You're gonna walk out of here with us like everything is normal. Got it?"

"Díaz, what are you doing?" The mustached man's gruff words returned a burst of oxygen to Cora's lungs. Would he help her?

"What does it look like?"

"We can't afford to kidnap someone right now."

"Maybe you can't." Díaz's grip on her arm cut tighter. "I can't go back to prison. We're getting out of here."

The older man cursed, making Cora wince.

Díaz dug the gun into her spine. "I'm gonna put this in my pocket, but my finger will be on the trigger the whole time. You talk or make a wrong move, and that security guard dies. And whatever other people I can take out before I go down. Got it?"

She moistened her lips as she darted her gaze around the baggage claim. There must be something she could do.

"Got it?" He jerked her arm. "Or I can start shooting right now."

"No." The word popped from her mouth with air she didn't know she had. "Don't hurt anyone. I'll go."

"Move." He released her arm, allowing blood and circulation to return with a surge of pain.

She walked toward the exit, Jana following at her side with her tail swishing as if it were the normal day it had been moments ago. *Please, Father. Don't let anyone get hurt. Show me what to do.*

If only she had made more headway with her proposal to the airport that metal detectors be installed at the baggage claim entrance. Most airports didn't have any such security measures in their arrivals area but Cora had been concerned about the vulnerability that created. And now a man had brought a gun in, just as she'd feared could happen someday.

Frank smiled as she neared.

The two men walked a few paces behind her.

Blood rushed in her ears. Should she run? Make a dash for the shuttle service counter near the doors and shout a warning to Frank?

Jana bumped lightly into Cora's leg as they walked.

No. Jana could get hurt. Frank could get shot. Anyone here could become a victim of her self-preservation.

She pasted on a smile and waved at Frank. "Have a good afternoon." Did her voice sound normal? It might have held a hint of the trembling that was now more constant than her breathing as fear took control of her body.

"You, too, Cora." Frank turned his head away as she passed through the doors.

Thank you, Lord. She must not have shown the growing terror that threatened to buckle her knees.

What would happen outside on the sidewalk? There were so many people. More than indoors but spread farther apart.

"Get in." Díaz cinched her arm in his grip again, standing too close. "Brown car."

She tried to swallow but coughed instead as frigid, January air broke into her lungs.

"Move." He pushed her forward, toward the empty brown four-door that waited by the curb. Waiting to take her. Where?

Jana nudged Cora's gloved hand with her nose.

Cora looked down at the beautiful golden's face, her hopeful gaze directed up at Cora. What would happen to Jana?

Never get in. Phoenix Gray's words blared through Cora's mind. How many times had Cora's employer told her this was where she was to draw the line? If anyone ever attempted to abduct her, she should do whatever it took to avoid getting into a vehicle. As the owner and founder of Phoenix K-9 Security and Detection Agency, Phoenix should know.

The mustached man opened the front passenger door and slipped inside as if he couldn't get away fast enough.

Díaz yanked open the back door. He started to push her inside.

She stiffened and pulled back.

Giggles.

She jerked her head to the left.

Three children hugged a suited man who kneeled on the sidewalk. He was likely their father, probably returned from a business trip.

"They'll be the first I'll shoot. Get in."

She couldn't risk that Díaz meant what he said. She turned back to Jana and the kidnapper's car. "In."

The golden jumped in easily at the command, as calm and steady as always.

Cora sat beside Jana on the backseat, her fingers shaking as she stroked the dog's fur. Thank the Lord Jana didn't have an ounce of guardian instinct, as her co-worker Bristol liked to joke. If she did, the men might have hurt her in their effort to kidnap Cora.

Or maybe...perhaps, Jana knew something Cora didn't. That there was nothing to fear.

As Díaz jerked the car into gear and pulled away from the curb, Cora's pulse pounded in her ears.

The remainder of Phoenix's repeated warning about abductions seared her thoughts.

If you get in, you're dead.

The greatest threat to this K-9 team is the one they don't see coming...

Cora Isaksson's guilt has shadowed her life ever since drugs ensnared her brother and he disappeared. When Bradley suddenly returns, Cora and her narcotics detection K-9 are thrust into a battle against the drug cartel that wants him back.

DEA Special Agent Kent Thomson has his own personal reasons for bringing justice to the cartel. Cora and her drug-sniffing K-9 will only get in his way. Or are they assets that will enable him to right the wrongs of the past?

When the cartel targets Cora, she and Kent join forces with her teammates at the Phoenix K-9 Security and Detection Agency to end the cartel before it ends her. They're prepared for danger, but when more lives than their own hang in the balance, can they trust God for the rescue that's out of their reach?

Shop *Hidden Danger* at
HiddenDangerBook.com

She never invites visitors. But visitors sometimes invite themselves.

When a winter storm brings more than snow, May Denver is forced to flee from her home and fight for her life. Can she trust an unwanted neighbor and risk her greatest fear in order to survive?

GRAB THIS ROMANTIC SUSPENSE STORY FOR FREE WHEN YOU SIGN UP FOR JERUSHA'S NEWSLETTER
www.FearWarriorSuspense.com

GUARDIANS UNLEASHED
"Fast-paced suspense at its best."
- DiAnn Mills,
bestselling author of Concrete Evidence
JERUSHA AGEN
RISING DANGER
JERUSHA AGEN
HIDDEN DANGER
JERUSHA AGEN
COVERT DANGER
JERUSHA AGEN
UNSEEN DANGER
JERUSHA AGEN
LETHAL DANGER
JERUSHA AGEN
TERMINAL DANGER
GuardiansUnleashed.com

It's up to a K-9 handler and her canine partner to stop a bomber before it's too late.

Shop the Guardians Unleashed Prequel Novel at
www.RisingDanger.com

The Sisters Redeemed Series

JerushaStore.com

ABOUT JERUSHA

Jerusha Agen imagines danger around every corner but knows God is there, too. So naturally, she writes romantic suspense infused with the hope of salvation in Jesus Christ.

Jerusha loves to hang out with her big furry dogs and little furry cats, often while reading or watching movies.

Find more of Jerusha's thrilling, fear-fighting stories at www.JerushaAgen.com.

facebook.com/JerushaAgenAuthor
instagram.com/jerushaagen